These Darker Streets

Abigail Linhardt

These Darker Streets

A SpaceDragon Creations book

This book is a work of fiction. Names, characters, places, and incidents either are the product of the author's imagination or are used fictitiously. Any resemblance to actual persons, living or dead, events, cultures, or locales is entirely coincidental.

Cover art by Popa Tudor. Chapter font by JosefinaTol.

Paperback ISBN: 978-1-957175-01-0

Harback ISBN: 978-1-957175-02-7

Also available in eBook and Audiobook from digital distributors.

ACKNOWLEDGMENTS

Special thank you to Laurie for her help in getting this second edition together. Wouldn't have done it if not for you!

Also, thank you to my readers for picking this up a second time and giving it another chance at life.

This story is for those who waited. To those who found out what love is. And to those who haven't.

These Darker Streets

Goddess Among Us Book 1

Abigail Linhardt

SpaceDragon Creations

CONTENTS

Chapter 1

Arawn

The streets of the small Ohio town glistened slick with cold rain as the man in the long coat and wide-brimmed hat ran down them. His long legs burned with the effort, and his lungs seared as he panted. The night had been quiet before, but when the howl of a hell hound broke his peaceful thoughts, he knew that danger lurked nearby. The man didn't try to dampen his booted footfalls; there was no point in trying to hide from this hunter.

He rounded a corner and stopped dead. His angled, dark eyebrows caved into a glare. At the end of the alley stood the hunter: Arawn and his shadow of a hound, fiery teeth bared.

"You run a good race, Ildanach," the older man said, his voice a deep echo in the quiet streets. "For too many years have you kept me out of this world. My dogs are hungry for mortal souls. It is the way of life. Why not let me go where I will, taking whom I will? Why do you insist on hindering me?"

Ildanach swallowed, trying to calm himself. "You take them before their time. Jennifer was not ready to die. She had years left!" Annoyance flooded him as his voice shook a little. He could not show weakness now. He must stay strong, protect this side of the veil where the mortals lived. "It has been my pleasure these last thousand years to ensure you don't take a single soul before it's time."

"It was her time!" Arawn screamed, his wrinkled face turned to a mask of loathing. "She was not the one you were looking for, Ildanach. You love too fast; you hope too much. You are foolish to think your power can keep me out."

Ildanach reached into his long coat and took out a small vial of glittering purple liquid. He uncorked it, his eyes never leaving the old man and the hound at the end of the street. Quickly, he shot the liquid back and reveled in its burn while the energy coursed instantly through his limbs.

"Still throwing back glow?" Arawn sneered. "That fairy potion will hardly make you strong enough to keep me out."

"I don't need to keep you out," Ildanach said. "I just need to keep the mortals safe."

"For another thousand years?" Arawn groaned. He patted his shadow hound on the head. "You grow weaker, I think. Why do you hold on to hope so?"

"To give mortals hope!" He cast a handful of iron dust at the old man and the hound yelped.

Iron poisoned the fairy people, even the darker ones like Arawn, the keeper of the underworld. With the distraction, Ildanach ran again, rejuvenated by the portion of his people: the immortal fairy beings from beyond the physical veil that separated the two worlds.

"There are better ways to take souls, Arawn," he shouted into the darkness as he ran. "This is the twenty-first century. No need for your hounds and this hunt you insist on."

Curious to see if Arawn followed him, Ildanach looked back just once. He could still see the outline of the hunter, but the hound disappeared. Fear put an extra stride in his already fast pace. He turned down an alley that would lead him to the main street where more lights and at least one bar were open, giving him some safety. Arawn never went where there were too many people. He usually exercised more caution with his soul-taking, despite his ravenous appetite for the chase.

But around the next corner, a heart-stopping bark made Ildanach slip on the wet street and fall directly onto his already sore backside. The hound leapt out of the street, fiery eyes and teeth snapping at his face. He cried out when the fangs latched onto his wrist as he tried to shield himself.

"I just wanted one soul," Arawn said softly, coming up from behind. "And I got hers. All I need is for you to lose hope. Without her, you cannot keep me out. And she's gone."

Jennifer had just been some girl he'd met, but he had thought she might be the one to heal the mortals of their despair and to love him, thus chaining Arawn and his hounds for another lifetime. But he made one mistake and her soul had been taken while he was away. She was gone and he had loved her.

Struggling as his own blood spattered his face, Ildanach tried to push the dark words from his mind. He had to get out of here. Something told him to run down the side street even though it yawned dark and seemingly deserted. Taking an iron knife from his belt, he stabbed the hound just once. It yelped and let go only to snap at his heels as he ran again.

"Run all you like, guardian!" Arawn called after him. "I have an eternity to fight you!"

The hound pursued him down the main street and into the dark alley that led to the next street over. The wounds had cost him dearly. They were healing already, but it had taken up most of the glow he had consumed just before. He tried to move his legs faster, Arawn's voice ringing in his ears. He ran often, hating it every time. He wanted to protect the mortals and his fellow immortals beyond the veil. Sometimes the choices were too hard to make.

He stopped in front of an exotic-looking store and took his sling from his belt. The hound homed in on him, its eyes fiery points down the alley. It stopped and growled, baring its teeth.

"Bad move," Ildanach grunted as he slung a perfect little iron stone at the monster. The stone grazed it enough to draw blood and anger the beast.

With a bark more like a roar, the hound charged. Ildanach loaded two stones this time and threw them hard from his sling. One slipped and shattered the window behind him and the other hit its mark. The beast fell to the ground, a smoking shadow just yards away from him.

He sighed in relief when he saw it take its last breath. Behind him, the alarm to the store had not gone off. Maybe the owner couldn't afford an alarm? Either way, the sign in the corner announced it would open in just a few hours at nine. He would need his companion, a sprite-goblin named Robin, and more glow to clean up the hellish mess the hound had left.

He took out his cell and dialed the number of his junkyard. He put his other hand, the injured one, on his hip and waited. He hated that junkyard, but living the life of a mortal came with some annoying bills. And buying glow from street fairies never came cheap either. Plus, the iron and other metals kept unwanted kith out.

He turned to the store as he left a voicemail - Robin still slept and didn't answer the phone. His eyes scanned the merchandise: Celtic knots, crystals, talismans, and runes glistened behind the window. It felt welcoming. After all, those were the symbols of his people. But there was no time. The sun rose without a care for his need, and the evidence of the violent world that surrounded the mortals every day needed to be cleared away before their innocent eyes saw the truth.

Chapter 2

This Immediate World

Brigit Elderbrook no longer wanted to live an extraordinary life. The dream of some kind of fantastic episode to change her life had never gone according to plan. It started when her father left her mother while she was still pregnant with her little brother, James. She had an older sister whom her father took with him, determined to groom her to take over as manager for his advertising firm once he retired. Brigit could not name one thing that made him leave, so assumed it must have been many. After all, her mother was an amazing woman. Why would anyone want to leave her?

Her mother had started her own business while pregnant with Brigit. A strange little store that sold Celtic charms and fairy paraphernalia by the basket load. Her mother fit into such a store perfectly with her long, sweeping red hair and charming, mysterious smile. She was very devout to all things mysterious and told fairy tales like some tell Bible stories. She brought Brigit up on the magic of witches and the lessons of toads. This upbringing made Brigit's imagination fly away. She loved the stories and had a heart full of hope and pixie dust as a child. But when her father left, she hated the powers on the other side of the fairy veil for not stopping him. Or turning him into a toad, or some other form of punishment. Life grew less and less magical as the years went on.

When James grew old enough for college, her mother had moved with him rather than letting him be on his own. Brigit volunteered to watch the store since she had received no job offers out of school and didn't want to take up her father's proposition in New York. She ignored his calls and only replied in short, quick sentences to his emails.

"I can't stomach the ethics of advertising," she had said crisply on their last phone call.

"Consumerism is the way of humankind," he had growled back. "Do you think people need that garbage your mother peddles?"

Somehow, the seclusion grew and soon, James and her mother didn't write as often and didn't call. She supposed they were busy with school things and left it alone. Part of her wanted to reach out again, but the other part liked the solitude. She had the store and a very loyal ferret named Henry.

The days of being alone passed when a businessman with one of the hundred-dollar haircuts "accidentally" hit her car one Sunday morning. He stepped out and pretended to stumble over his words.

"Oh hell, I've done it." He flicked his oiled bangs out of his face and smiled when Brigit ran out to the front, her mouth agape at the scrape. "I'm so sorry, miss." he said, coming to her.

"It was parked," she said, trying to let him know how stupid she thought he was. "How did you even hit it?"

He smiled. All his teeth were even, white, and shiny. "I was too distracted by a fire inside the window of your shop." He swiped vigorously on his phone while speaking.

"What?" she glanced back. No fire blazed inside; just a reflection of her in her oversized sweater and red hair. The sun shining on it made it look like a smoldering fire. "Oh, haha, very funny." She patted her hair. She hadn't brushed it that morning. The days were giving her less and less reason to even do that much.

"I try," he replied, his hands on his hips now as he smoothly slid the phone into his back pocket. "So, to make up for it, want to go get some coffee?" He pointed to the coffee shop across the way.

She should have thought harder; thought of her car that no doubt watched her flirt, disappointed in how quickly she forgot about it. But what did she have to lose?

"Why not. It's a cold morning, anyway."

And he'd be paying, right?

Her friend Mary, the owner of the shop, watched them come in and blessedly didn't say anything. Her body froze and her eyes tracked him like a hawk, a tiny and wicked grin dancing in the shadow of her cool face. She knew that if Brigit came in with a guy, it meant magic was happening. She'd sworn off dating since their family split up and had only a few casual encounters since. Mary always tried to get her to go out, but

Brigit made up a new excuse every time. Usually having to do with men being rats, or there was no such thing as true love.

"Two red eyes, please," the man said as he tipped Mary generously. "So, firebird, what is it you sell in there?"

"Um." Brigit pushed her hair behind one ear. "Just fairy trinkets, incense, dragon-themed stuff, Wiccan supplies - that kind of thing."

"Sounds crazy," he said, handing her a drink.

Brigit caught Mary as she mouthed behind her hand, "He's hot!" Brigit rolled her eyes and led him to a table far away from the counter.

"It is a little crazy, I guess," she stammered. "It was my mom's shop, but she moved down south to be with my brother."

"So, does it make you enough money to live on? I mean, that kind of thing can't be too popular." He took a drink and checked his watch.

She frowned at the intrusive device. "Sort of. I have other options in marketing. It's what I went to school for, but I don't like it that much."

"Big businesses hire marketing girls." He winked at her. "And you have a lot going for you." He reached over and touched her palm with his soft fingers. "My business is looking for people in marketing with your..." his eyes wandered over her, "with your qualifications."

This had turned into a bad idea. She snatched her hand away. "How do you know my qualifications?"

"Internet, sweet thing!" he beamed as though he had just done a fantastic magic trick. "I saw your profile online and thought, 'Damn, why is this woman not working for me?'"

"Because I like my shop!" she protested. She also made a

mental note to check her security settings online and any old desperate attempts she had made on job sites months ago. He must have read her pleading cover letter. Something written by a young, naive girl desperate for a job and to prove herself in big business. This was not her anymore.

"No, you don't." He locked his icy eyes on her. "Look, I can get you a good job, and with your talent, you'll move up in the ranks. Get an office close to mine." He let that hang in the air while she decided on what he meant by it.

Disgusted, she pushed away to leave. He stood up first. "Alright, I get it. Don't say I didn't try, firebird." He winked at her and walked out the door just as Mary brought their check over.

Brigit moaned and put her face in her hands. Her car was scraped, she looked desperate, and the drinks were on her.

"Don't worry," Mary shrugged, tearing up the bill. "He ran off before I made him pay."

"He was fast," Brigit sighed. She rubbed her temples. "Who am I fooling, anyway? I'm stuck in this little shop in this little town and I'm not trying to get out." She sighed again. "I have to go open my doors."

Mary gave her one last hug and Brigit went to her own shop. She opened the curtains and let the sunlight in. The golden rays streamed into her darkest corners where piles of dragons stared down from various shelves. She dusted off the walls and re-organized her blessed candles before her phone rang. Curious that her cell chirped and not the store phone, she answered it.

"Is this Brigit Elderbrook?" a friendly grandmother-like voice said.

"Yes," she replied, hoping this wasn't some trick from the business guy. "What can I help you with?"

"I'm sorry to inform you of this, but you were the only contact listed on Ondine Elderbrook's emergency information."

"What's happened?" Brigit asked. "Is mom alright?"

"I'm sorry, Miss Elderbrook, but you mother and brother James were in a car accident."

Brigit's heart stopped and her ears rang as if the woman had shouted the words. She should have texted James back sooner. He had sent her a picture of him in his football jersey just the day before. Just hours ago, it seemed. She didn't reply, knowing he'd wait for her words. It was the first text he'd sent in months. She had bet the jersey smelled like new plastic and rubber. He played college football? Amazing. She would have seen his games. Cheered him on.

The woman still talked and said something about immediate cremation being in her mother's will.

"So, I can't even see them?" she whispered weakly.

"Well, the will was dated nearly three years ago, and your signature is on it, too. Was that the last time you were together with your mother? We need to know for legal reasons."

Brigit closed her eyes as she admitted it. "Yes. It's been almost three years. Just over two, actually. Maybe. I don't know."

Why had she not been closer to her mother and brother?

No, magic did not exist in this world. Just death and ratty businessmen. And now she had a job to do. She had to organize a funeral and get all the legal work settled. And she'd have to call her father.

Life walked so imminently with death. Between the two came just the work you did to pass the time. And this was one of those pieces of work you did.

"I can handle all the arrangements," Brigit said at last. She was strong, she could do this.

Chapter 3

This Life

Brigit tried to be thankful to the sun's appearance as she walked from the parking garage to her shop on the backstreet. The garage was for business owners and a better option after the scrape with the creepy guy. Ohio didn't see sun much this time of year and she wanted to be grateful. She had the most bizarre dream about being in Stonehenge the night before, and the eerie music and dancing figures were still vivid in her eyelids. She didn't want to dwell on the terrors, images, and nightmares. After all, life had been all funeral preparations and grey skies since the accident. She glared at her coffee mug that had a stupid smiling flower on it. Yes, she would make the best of today.

Her heart and her face fell when she came to her store front. The glass, shattered, sparkled over the floor, and the alarm failed to go off again. Praying nothing had been taken, she unlocked the door in haste. She couldn't afford the insurance on the window, so losing merchandise would have really ruined her day. She rushed around the whole store to make sure everything was fine. To her surprise, and as though the Powers That Be realized she was already having a bad day, nothing was missing.

"Oh, Henry!" she cried when she spotted a little cage behind the cash wrap. Inside, her little white ferret, Henry, poked his head out of his hammock. His eyes wide, he seemed to say, "Yes, mistress? What troubles you?" rather than condemning her for forgetting to take him home. She brought him to work as she normally turned off the heat in the apartment when gone to save expenses. Perhaps the time came to move back into the loft over the store.

"I'm sorry I forgot you, but I had to pick up the flowers this morning and I was just so messed up when the florist said, 'Try something brighter'. You know, it's a funeral."

She put up the play pen and let him do his business in the little litter box in the corner. Before opening up the box the florist had suggested, she paused to look in the huge magic mirror hanging on her wall. An expensive thing to order, she thought someone would buy it, but no luck yet. Maybe everyone else caught on to the phony magic.

Long, frizzy red hair and tired eyes reflected back at her. She put on weight these days faster than she realized. After the accident, she didn't have the strength to make the wholesome food her mother used to and bake pies. Her idea of dessert these days were those artificial pies that came in tiny boxes from the gas station.

"I look like James," she said to Henry behind her, who happily played with his rubber ball, glad to have his toy at last. "Sometimes, I can't remember mom at all, and it's only been a few weeks." She stared at herself. "I can't remember anything these days," she moaned. A fresh wave of crying built up in her chest. *Damn, this crying thing!* She cried all the time now.

She got a broom from the closet and began to sweep up the glass. "Who'd break a window and not steal anything?" she sighed, the tears coming any way. "Why do something so stupid? Just to ruin my life even more? Just take the whole damn store while you're at it! Take everything!"

She had to stop and breathe. This was silly. She was losing it, and it wasn't even nine in the morning yet. She picked up a crystal ball and balanced it in the palm of her hand. She used to love visiting psychics and having her fortune read. She loved fairy tales and stories about 'once upon a time' that ended with happily ever after. But those were all so fake. Nothing in this world gave hope, made one feel loved - everything nine-to-five, bills, dirty streets, and car accidents due to people driving intoxicated. And dead mothers and brothers. That was life.

She gently eased the ball down. The fault didn't rest on one person, really. Maybe she should blame her father for running off and taking her older sister with him. Maybe blame the teenagers who were driving high for homecoming who crashed into her mother's car. Maybe blame herself for not going out to the movie with them. Maybe the last thing she said to her brother ruined her memories. Maybe anything could be blamed - everything could be.

After sweeping up the glass and tossing it out, she put a huge Celtic blanket over the hole to cover the wood she propped up to keep out the evil wind. Then she opened the register to count the money and get ready for the day. Before she mentally prepared herself, the time had come to face the flowers in the box the florist sent over. She had loved flowers once. Now they were harbingers of doom.

Inside, a nice letter written in the curly scrawl of the energetic florist read: "Dear Miss Elderbrook, please accept our apologies for the first arrangement. We were not aware how you felt about roses, but when you said you wanted something different, that was our first try. Please see the enclosed arrangement free of charge and..." It went on and on.

She stared at the flowers for a good ten minutes when a cry of "Holy Anubis!" alerted her to her ever-faithful friend Mary. She smiled as Mary let herself in.

"Someone robbed you last night?" she gasped, pushing her hair behind her ear and readjusting the black-rimmed glasses. She had an attractive librarian look to her that Brigit had always been jealous of. Mary handed her a nice, hot Chai latte.

"No," Brigit replied. "They just smashed my window for the fun of it." They silently stared at it for a moment.

Mary turned to Brigit with bright eyes. "Well, I know you don't have that covered by insurance, so..." she waited dramatically. "Have you thought about that meditation and essential oils class I asked you to teach for me in the loft? Five dollars a head. You can have a share of tickets and any drink sales that night. C'mon."

Mary owned the coffee shop across the street from Brigit's store and had a loft above that she rented out to artsy types who wanted to host a gallery or a special class. Brigit made her own recipes and mixes of essential oils and was well-versed in a special highbred kind of meditation that involved the Celtic Triskelion. Mary had been trying to host her for months.

"I'm not feeling very calm and meditative these days," Brigit said after a sip of her latte. "Not sure I can do one more thing along with this funeral. And I have to go meet my dad this weekend."

"Oh, sorry about that. But you're right," Mary added quickly. "I mean, what was I thinking? Do you need help with that? I should have asked earlier."

Brigit shook her head. "Just keep the Chai coming and I'll be fine."

"Oh Ra," Mary sighed. She clutched her ankh around her neck in a tight fist. "That old fart and his dog are back. Taking a poop right in the only patch of grass for a mile."

Outside, an old man in a trench coat and his fluffy white dog stood near the little square of grass that had a stunted tree growing out of it right in front of the store. The dog sniffed, squatted, and did his business. The man walked away without picking it up.

"Want me to call the city officials?" Mary offered.

"Nope," Brigit sighed, pulling on the gloves she kept for cleaning up after Henry. "I'm used to dealing with shit."

She picked up the tiny poop, sure that Henry's were larger and less smelly, and disposed of it outside.

"Now is that so hard?" she asked her friend once they were safe back inside. "So, you'll never guess what I'm deciding to do between now and burying the ashes."

Mary frowned and nodded, looking at herself in the mirror and measuring her bust size. "I meant to ask if you cremated. I thought it would be too soon."

Brigit cleared her throat and bounced on the balls of her feet, staring down. Mary took the sign to hush up. "They were just too...they needed to be. The accident was just so..." She put her face in her hands. She should have visited them more in the last three years. The guilt ate her away, weakening her body and her mind.

"So, tell me what you've decided to do," Mary prompted, taking her friend's hand, and massaging it.

"Columbus," Brigit said quickly, dropping her other hand. "The Pagan Fantasy Convention?" She tossed an elaborately illustrated pamphlet onto the counter. It had been read often, evidenced by the fraying edges and faded spots.

"You're going to Fantasy Con?" Mary beamed, her face alight with joy. "You'll love it! Maybe you can pick up some stuff there to suit my people more?" She twirled the golden ankh around her neck. "Maybe add a little flavor to this Pictish warrior place of yours."

"I am going to find new things." She looked around. "Yeah, this place needs new stuff. All of this," she waved her hand, "it's all mom. I've been running it, but I haven't brought in anything new. I guess it was my way to be with her even though she was states away."

"I think you're making a superb choice. Getting new things will be good." Mary took her friend's hand again. "But that is soon, right?"

Brigit nodded. "Everything seems to be coming before I'm ready."

Chapter 4

Lifting The Veil

Brigit stared at the flowers on her desk as some curious people walked past her shop. The people who went to the gym down the road at ungodly hours always peeked in her window, but never came in. She had teenagers, worried women, and men who smelled like too much frankincense come in. Every once in a while, a "normal" person interested in fantasy or Wicca stopped by, but normally the days were slow. She had filled them up with anxiety and depression recently.

"This is the rose arrangement the place sent," she said, tweaking one of the flowers. She sighed again.

"Those sighs are getting deeper and longer," Mary pointed out. "This one looks like Valentine's Day."

Brigit smiled. "Right? I wonder what mom would say."

"James wouldn't like it."

She nodded. Her brother had been such a manly boy. Always tried to be, but he was just too sweet. "I may keep it, but I don't know. Help me, here."

Just then, the tiny little chimes above the door tinkled as the

first customer of the morning stepped in. Brigit ignored him at
first, but Mary's jabbing and strained squeaks finally got her
attention.

She hissed at her friend silently, then looked up. The man
was not overly tall, but stood head and shoulders above Brigit.
His hair gleamed soft and brushed his shoulders in clean, dark
waves. His eyes shimmered brown and had a slightly sprite-like
quality; sweet mischief lurked just underneath. But all this
encased in deep brown eyes set in a strong brow. He would have
looked younger except for the dark bristles along the lower
portion of his face. He possessed a perfect combination of
manly and playful. Brigit tried not to eye him, but his sturdy
frame and lithe hands looked powerful with their long fingers.

He half smiled when he saw her looking at him and stupidly
blinking back. She tried to look away again, but a talisman
around his neck caught her eye: a little green stone pierced by a
silver sword.

Mary elbowed her hard when neither of them spoke.

"What can I help you find?" Brigit coughed suddenly.

"Um," he said unexpectedly. His voice deep and smooth
like a river stone. "Sorry about your window."

"You know something about that?" Brigit suddenly perked
up. "It was broken this morning."

He shook his head, his hair glinting in the sun. "Uh, no, I
just noticed it was broken, is all." He ran his hand through his
hair and placed his other on his well-muscled hip. He had a
thick black belt on under his long coat with a triskelion buckle.
He laughed and shook his head. "I was looking for a talisman."

"I like the one you have," Brigit said. "What's it mean? I'm
not familiar with it."

"Oh, uh," he fumbled with it and laughed again. "It's something I made a long time ago. Kind of a symbol of the earth," he pointed to the stone, "and the sword represents the guardian, protecting her."

"Ah," Brigit nodded. "Just so you know, I sell this stuff, but I don't believe in it."

He stopped and locked eyes with her. His were so dark as she looked deeper. And deeper. They were black holes: no end to his gaze, eternal and warm. She almost actually felt herself sinking when he said, "Well, I'll just look around then."

"Mighty Bast," Mary gasped. She never ran out of Egyptian deities to swear by. "Look at that."

"Shush!" Brigit snapped. "He can probably still hear you."

"Tall, dark hair, dark eyes, and that coat is doing wonders to his body."

Brigit glanced quickly at his back as he examined some crystals. "What's your point?"

"Well," she sipped her tea. "I didn't see a ring. Maybe he can help you, you know, take your mind off things." She wiggled her eyebrows quickly and smiled over her cup.

Realizing what her friend suggested, Brigit rolled her eyes and unpacked some new merchandise. "No, I can't. Do you know what that would mean - putting aside this funeral like that?" Her heart ached again, and her emotions got the better of her. "I can't do that, Mary, okay? It's only been a few weeks. They were my world. My everything! They gave me hope and let me dream up a new life when this one got me down. They were there for me for everything!"

"Brig," Mary tried to cut in, seeing the danger signs.

"No, I just can't. They're dead and I need to deal with that first!"

Silence fell except for the little wishing well near the front door that trickled without a care in the world. The man watched her too. She sighed and covered her face. How idiotic could she be? Why had she lost her temper like that? Why could Mary not understand what was going on in her life right now?

When she looked up, the man stood at the register.

"I'll take this one." He placed a crystal down. The tag read, "To guard against the sorrow of loss."

Really? Brigit thought to herself. Out loud she said, "Suppose I need one, huh?"

The man watched her with sympathetic eyes. It made them all the deeper and more gorgeous. "I too have lost someone recently. I thought she was everything. I miss her, but I know she's in a better place right now. Even though it's not with me."

Brigit tried to laugh, but it came out as a grunting sneer. "The afterlife. Not something I think about anymore."

"Why not?" he asked. No rush or accusation infected his tone.

"You're really going to make me talk about this?" She raised her eyebrows and told him the total. "My mom and brother were good people. I hadn't seen them in years, yeah, but they were good. They didn't deserve this. If there is some afterlife, and a host of ethereal beings watching over us, then why did that happen? Where was their guardian angel?"

"How can you sell hope and magic and not believe in it?" he asked simply. "Don't you dream anymore, Brigit?"

Her mouth almost smiled when she heard the way her name

sounded in his voice. It sounded right. She took her name tag off. "I'm more of a realist. This stuff just lets people forget about how dark and bad the world is."

"And this?" he tapped the brochure to the convention she had left lying on the counter. "Why here then?"

Brigit snatched the brochure up and tossed it under the register. "I have to go. For the store." How dare he judge her! He knew nothing about her and tried to pry out her secrets and feelings.

He smiled at her. She tried to glare back, proving her strength, but his face disarmed her. His eyes smiled when his mouth did, and his hair shone brighter. It had been a long time since she'd seen a genuine smile like that.

"I need you to order another talisman that you're out of," he said gently.

"I can't order right now," she snapped.

He took the crystal. "Right. Well, I'm sorry about the window." With long strides, he passed through the door and dissipated into the sunshine on the pavement.

Brigit shook her head. "He was weird."

Chapter 5

The Guardian

Ildanach tried not to walk too fast as he left the store. He clutched the crystal in his fingers until it hurt and didn't loosen his grip until seated on his big, old Ducati. He breathed in and out slowly, placing the crystal around his neck. That girl, Brigit the name tag read, was a spout of energy. He could see it emanating from her practically. But it wasn't good. Anger and confusion permeated her aura. He could see that. Behind all that, a gaping well of loneliness waited to be filled. She hid it well, expertly almost, not letting anyone else see it. Almost too good at hiding and putting on her strong mask. Something else radiated inside her. Something he hadn't seen in a mortal woman for many, many years. A kind of glowing spark pulsating, waiting to be awakened.

Because of the obvious magic emanating from her, the way she talked about it bothered him. She had a flare to her he thought had been her glowing faith - he had been wrong. Her essence held a fairy-like sparkle he realized he must have misread. Still, the glow shined in her, despite her dark spirit. Jennifer hadn't had that glow. He hadn't seen a glow like that in years.

Even without the mysterious aura, the woman was beautiful. She didn't dress like regular mortals and had an air about her that vibrated calm and unconcerned - a control. He wished he could break from it. Thousands of years of being guardian to the earth could be trying at times.

His garage and junkyard sprawled out across the land he owned, a vast playground of every kind of car imaginable. Through some powers of his own, he acquired a plethora of parts, including some from the 1920s and some very brightly colored foreign cars. He hardly knew everything that he had - that job belonged to Robin. The little pixie-goblin had been an excellent records keeper and had talked Ildanach into using the glow's power to acquire some of the rarer parts.

"I was waiting for breakfast, but no!" the little pixie shouted from behind a car he was repairing for a customer. He was welding on a new piece and didn't have a mask on to protect his huge, green eyes.

"My morning was great," Ildanach said as he flipped off the loud radio. "I didn't even have to exile anyone. Ran into some hell hounds, though. And a, uh, shop keeper. When was that mortal convention Herne said he'd be at?"

"Thanks for asking how my morning went," Robin sighed as he hefted some tires up onto the shelf, abandoning the welding now. "I was asked again if I was the god Pan by a small mortal."

"They were asking if you were *Peter Pan*," Ildanach mumbled, correcting his friend before his head swelled. "Biiiiig difference." He put an oil funnel on Robin's head as he passed and laughed as the sprite stumbled. "Let's not go about thinking you're bigger than you are."

"Five-one!" Robin grunted. "You and your tallness wouldn't know anything about it."

"Six-three," he said. "Really, why do I have you if you can't keep any facts straight? How will my business ever run? Now, convention?"

"Sign up was last month or something," he said, digging oil out from under his nails and tilting the oil funnel to a jaunty angle rather than taking it off. "Herne asked if you'd go to keep an eye on some really active love-spirits who were going to attend." He grinned, a twinkle in his eyes. "Why do you want to go all of a sudden? Thought you told Herne to buzz off. Or—if I must stick to the facts—you said, 'Shove your antlers up your ass, I'm not going. Send some other fairy.'"

Ildanach laughed and pulled his hair up into a ponytail. "That's not verbatim what I told the horned god. I need to go. To, uh, check something out."

Robin watched his master with quizzical eyes. He could tell he hid something, but it wasn't his place to interfere. "Speaking of magic," he bit at his little pixie nails. "You know, with our magic, we could easily run a huge business; take over some corporation. I mean, this is the twenty-first century - let's live a little. This laying low in grease is bad for my skin. Eh?"

Ildanach didn't listen. The newspaper that had once again landed in a splat of oil that morning caught his eyes. It wasn't the city newspaper; no, that brought only boring news. This one, the tabloid, brought news that interested him - most of the news of the fairy activity ended up in there. The headline blasted in huge black letters something about a gargoyle rampaging through a small town just outside the nearest corn field towards Wakshaw, the county just south of them.

"Robin, what have you heard from the others recently?" he said, picking up the paper. "Anything going on?"

"Well, glow is getting scarce." This news he'd been saving all morning and still Ildanach didn't turn his eyes up. "Ildanach, not a lot of glow left. Hello? I also heard you got tongue-tied over some shop keeper."

Ildanach's head snapped up. He tried to frown. His eyebrows twitched and soon he smiled. "I can't figure out what it is about her. She's so angry, yet so full of life. She has a hope inside her I can see. She fights it."

Robin rolled his large eyes. "That is way too many contradictions for me. The gargoyle actually hit town this morning." He changed topics quickly. Women were a touchy subject still. He wondered how Ildanach coped with the loss. Especially since it involved fairy activity. He hadn't dared ask yet. "It was sniffing around Main Street. Near her shop," he added when Ildanach seemed to need more prodding.

"Of course. Thanks, Robin!"

"But breakfast!" the pixie pleaded.

Ildanach had already yanked his wide-brimmed hat onto his head and took up his belt hung with special artifacts for hunting such things. He didn't want to kill it - no, it was innocent so far - he wanted to make sure it stayed that way. And would maybe get a second glance at Brigit while out. He had to know if what he had spotted was real or not. In the fairy world, the one that existed in the same time and place as the mortal one, on another plane, each being had a little fire inside them that grew and glowed, fueled by the hope and faith of mortals. Brigit had something similar inside her. He was sure of it.

He had to quickly put the shop keeper out of his head when he realized he had driven most of the way to Main Street. He double-checked to make sure he had his supplies. He had left without thinking. She intruded on his thoughts too much. He couldn't afford to make mistakes. Not with Arawn prowling the mortal's world like never before.

Ildanach made some rounds of the streets, trying to avoid the shop, but he couldn't. He drove past her store probably ten times before the traffic light blessedly turned red and allowed him to watch her for a few minutes while he sat at the crossroads. He saw her fiery hair through the glass on the other side he hadn't smashed that morning. She kept busy, and he noticed the flowers were now proudly displayed on the front register. She must have decided to like them. He wondered about the girl she hid behind a mask from the world. Wondered if she really did still want to believe in magic. His kind of magic.

He stalled out his bike when the car behind him shrieked a honk and he tried to slam on the gas. His motorcycle backfired and made a dog nearby bark. Panicking, he started it again and sped off, expertly weaving through traffic to reach the alley he knew the gargoyle would hang out in. He'd guessed where it hid for some time; he just didn't want to deal with it while a chance of seeing Brigit remained.

He parked and made his way quickly down the alley to the old abandoned Catholic church where the thing slept in the sun on the front, blending in perfectly. Glancing around to make sure he wouldn't be seen; he hefted the stone statue up and carried it inside. The weight made him groan as his back strained. This was his job: to protect both sides and make sure everyone behaved themselves.

He put the gargoyle down in the confessional where the sun couldn't touch it and it immediately sprang to life, hissing and baring its fangs.

"Be still!" Ildanach hissed and touched it with an iron rod. The thing roared and tried to slash at him with its long claws. Years of experience allowed Ildanach to dodge most of the attempts. When his purple blood showed, the beast calmed a bit and glared at Ildanach in confusion. "I am one of you," he said. "I am not here to kill; just answer my questions."

"A hunter you are, but my blood it is naught. You have come to inquire and to be taught," the creature said softly.

Ildanach could tell it was an old beast from the way it spoke. "You need to spend more time outside," he said, releasing it. "Get to know modern day speech better."

The gargoyle hummed and grunted. "I try, I do. The glow is scarce."

"That's better." He leaned against the side of the confessional. "Now, tell me about the glow. Why is it not being brought into the cities anymore?"

"The fairies don't want it. Losing hope, like humans do. No more powers. Just eternity."

Ildanach frowned. His people were losing hope? How could that be? Was it contagious? Were the humans picking up on it too? "What about Arawn? Tell me about him."

"The master of the underworld seeks new thrills," the gargoyle said. "Puts thoughts in their heads, gives them chills. Only souls of the darkest color can be taken down into his harbor."

Ildanach stood up. "Over my dead body."

"That may be the dark one's idea." The gargoyle yawned

dramatically and scratched his ear like a dog. "Plant the fear, no magic will appear. Easy souls." He blinked slowly. "Not worth it, these mortals, guardian. Why not fade, go away? Let them not believe."

Ildanach shoved open the door and raced out to his motor-cycle. He had discovered Arawn's game. The master of the underworld wanted to drive fear into mortal souls. Why? What happened that would force Arawn to make ripples in the mortal pond? Ildanach didn't want to take violent actions. If he had to, he might. He had to protect the mortals.

His phone buzzed in his pocket.

A text from Robin: *Others saw Arawn leave. Took all hounds. Probably gone for the weekend. All is safe.*

Ildanach let his face fall into a rare, concentrated frown. "For now."

Chapter 6

Together

Brigit took her car the whole way to Columbus, not wanting to depend on public transportation. Besides, she had some promises to keep. Her mother, a fanatic of all things fantasy, loved this con and went whenever the family could afford it. She had always tried to get Brigit to go, but school and work were simple, wonderful excuses to avoid it. Now Brigit realized she'd been lying all that time. She loved the world her mother lived in; however, make-believe made an unhealthy diet. Like eating cake all the time. Part of her wanted it to be real, and the idea seemed whimsical and fun. She had to be careful. She knew that if she went in too deep, she may not come out again.

She had thought about it for years now. She had compiled a list of songs to listen to in order to get in the mood. She needed to be open-minded and have a clear head to order new merchandise for her shop. The artists were always good at these kinds of things. She also needed to have a sense of what she wanted to put into the store. She wanted to be inspired and enjoy herself.

The emotions kept washing around inside of her, making it difficult.

The parking garage proved to be a labyrinth, packed with teenagers in strange robes with staves, long hair, fairy wings attached by wires, fake elf ears, and some undefinable in monster-like garb. She would never have the nerve to dress up like that. Even the goth kids in their black and colored hair with their large pentagrams were weird to her. Nope, she liked normal things. Normal was good.

Parking took longer than she thought and before she knew it, she was late for the first event she wanted to see. A woman specializing in dragons presented her newest work and gave away advanced reader copies of her illustrated book to merchants and she wanted to get one.

She crammed herself into an already over-packed elevator to take her to the first floor where the large conference room hosted the event. Someone smelled like too much patchouli, and another smelled like a lack thereof. She sighed, anxious to get out. Why did she come? Surely she could find new and interesting merchandise online. Cheaper too. Crappier. She wanted to slap herself. This was a bad idea.

When the doors opened, she stampeded her way out first and ran to the great golden doors in front of her. A security guard outside stopped her.

"Event started fifteen minutes ago, and they have instructed us not to let anyone in after."

"Ugh, why?" This trip steadily got worse.

The guard shrugged but didn't move.

"I need to be in there though."

"I'm sorry ma'am." He didn't even look it.

She had dragged a small backpack on wheels all the way through the parking lot, passing the weirdos, and into that elevator for nothing. She walked away to find an information boot and get a schedule.

"Tell me there is something open," she said through gritted teeth to the attendant behind the table.

"Well," the bookish little girl said brightly. "Everything for the first hour is in session. If you'd like, there are vendors setting up in the main hall. They should be ready within the hour. And then at ten, the rooms will open again."

"Ugh!" she moaned. "Fine, where is the main hall?"

"I can show you," said a playful, deep voice behind her. "I know all the secret little places that are the best."

She spun around and came face-to-face with the man from before. He smiled, his hands tucked in his front pockets. It did not surprise her to see him among the dressed-up crowd. He wore a black velvet magus robe and a wide, black hat with one side pinned up by a huge, gaudy green gem. She wanted to turn her nose up at his clothes, even though they made it so she couldn't stop from looking. The clothes fit him snuggly and well.

"Of course, you do," she said at last. "Why are you here?"

He laughed lightly. Then, watching her closely, he said "My name's Ildanach." When she replied with a pretentious brow raise and nothing more, he went on more casually. "I come here every year. We just established that. I have a *lot* of weird friends I need to get in touch with. This is the place to find them."

"Right." That statement came out far more loaded than she meant it to be, and he could tell.

"Come on." He held a hand to her, but she didn't take it.

Instead, he smiled again, glowing, and led her down to a huge hallway where vendors were indeed setting up.

"Not the cosplaying type?" he asked simply, looking over at her. He seemed to make more eye contact than normal people.

"Left my costume at home," she tried.

"Sure." He nodded, his long hair brushing his shoulders. He walked closer to where she stood. "I'm fascinated by how you talked about not liking this kind of thing, yet you're here."

She shrugged, leaning against the wall next to him. "For the store. I'm here as a merchant, for your information. I'm not a hypocrite."

"I'd never think that. I'm just fascinated." He tilted his head to catch her eyes again. "I like people with more than one side."

Meeting his eyes brought a small smile to her face. "Well, I think you're weird." She closed her eyes in embarrassment.

"What I mean is -"

"I know what you mean," he laughed. "You're dark, tortured, and brooding and I'm imaginative and strange."

She raised her eyebrows. "You are confident."

"Let me show you a favorite of mine." He walked to a vendor that just opened and picked up a small book in leather binding. "This is the story of the Lily Maid and Lancelot."

"I thought Lancelot loved Guinevere," she said, hovering close to his arm to see the book in his hand as he flipped through.

"Ah, that was the forbidden love. You like that story?"

She rolled her eyes. "Tell me this one."

"Well, Elaine was trapped in a tower, and she was cursed to not look out the window."

"Or what? She'd die?"

Ildanach smiled. "As curses often go, yes. She had a mirror that showed her the world. It reflected what was outside the window. As we all know, a reflection is not as good as the real thing. It's all backwards; maybe out of focus."

"Oh," she hummed. She tried to not see her life in that analogy. "So, what happened?"

Ildanach turned the page to a beautiful image of a knight in shiny armor. "Lancelot came by her window. She saw him in the mirror and had to turn to see him for herself."

"So, some hottie walks by, and she loses it?"

"You really are the stoic," he laughed, tucking his hair behind one ear. "No, you see, she was destined to love him."

He put the book down and pulled her to the next table. There were hair pieces, crowns, bracelets, and rings all bearing magic symbols. He picked up a wire laurel made of lilies with long white, pink, and green ribbons hanging down the back. He faced her, brushed her hair back from her face, letting his fingers linger just a moment too long on her temple before setting the laurel on her head.

"You could be the Lily Maid."

"No, I don't believe in love at first sight either." She took the laurel off and plucked at some talismans instead. Those might work for her store. Her face burned with an unknown fire. His dark eyes had looked into hers. It her stomach flip like the first drop on a rollercoaster.

"What do you believe in, Brigit?" he crossed his arms and leaned on the table.

"This." She pulled out her wallet. "How much for bulk order of your purple talismans?" she asked the vendor.

"I can't deny it's usefulness," he replied. "I don't think Elaine had any in the tower. She did other things."

"Like what? Weave images all day she could never see? Dream her life away and never try to escape? The bitch was lame."

Ildanach pushed off the table, standing up straight. "You *did* know the story?" He didn't sound angry at her, more fascinated that she said nothing.

"Look, I'm sorry. I can't make excuses for my behavior recently. I've had a lot on my mind."

She almost expected him to say he understood and leave her alone. Instead, he smiled warmly again, causing hot vibrations to run up and down her whole body.

"I always blamed Lancelot," Ildanach said instead. "I mean, what was he doing by a cursed tower, anyway? It had been there for decades. He had to have known what was up."

"Maybe he wasn't into everyone else's business. Besides, he said when she was dead that she went to heaven when all the other men thought she was damned for sure."

"You like Lancelot, the man who stole the king's bride, over poor, innocent Elaine?" His joking sounded so cynical it actually made her laugh.

"I haven't read legends like that in a long time," she sighed, moving on to the next table. This one had art and paintings. "I used to love them. Now I couldn't tell you what half of these are. Oh!"

She scooped up a painting and cooed again. "Look! A ferret in armor!"

Ildanach stood behind her. The warmth from his tall, solid body kissed her skin through her thins shirt. She caught his scent for the first time: fire, spices, and something sweet. She exhaled, calming her mind.

"You like those little things, don't you?" he asked. She could hear the warm smile in his tone.

"Well, Henry is a prince, and I treat him so bad sometimes. He deserves better." She smiled at the painting. It would be just for her. She liked it and realized she hadn't bought herself anything in a long time. She came here for the store. To make that part of her life better.

"No, I should focus," she said, putting it down. "Show me those good vendors."

They spent the next few hours taking cards and samples from other vendors of strange and curious things she found interesting. Ildanach liked watching her here. She became livelier, more curious than the girl he had met before as they investigated vendors. The girl he met in the shop had a kind of beauty, was full of life, but also stifled it so roughly he thought she'd explode. This new light enticed him in a way he thought he'd forgotten.

Brigit was oblivious to his eyes. She thought she caught him looking at her more than once and ignored it. She didn't know why she pushed it away so strongly. She just knew that now was not the time for such an emotional infatuation. No matter how deep and brown his eyes were. No matter how much his smile made her toes curl in excitement. Besides, he behaved far too plucky for a man.

"Do you have a pet?" she asked as they packed up some new tapestries she ordered. He had been helping her carry new merchandise all day and never complained once.

"I have an associate who may as well be a pet. He eats all

my food and rents a room from me. He does good work though. His name's Robin."

She laughed at his wit, then cleared her throat and focused ahead. What was she doing? He must have cast a spell on her. Making her heart light, her mind clear, and she had not laughed this much in years. She needed to change tactics. Something to ground her.

"Are you married or seeing anyone?" There, that would do it. A stone dropped into her stomach when she asked, and her heart begged him to say no. Not that she would do anything about him being single. Still...

"Um, no. I was seeing someone once. It was a while ago though. A long time ago, actually." Even though memories darkened his face, his eyes were still warm. Would nothing faze him? Did anything bring him down? He was strange in that way, she decided. Who had this much happiness in them? This much patience. Especially for her and her moping and snapping.

"You?" he asked.

"Tch," she said too quickly. "No. I can't decide."

"On what?" he laughed.

She frowned, honestly thinking. "On if it's worth it or not. Investing the time, the emotion, the passion. Everything. It's a big deal." She shrugged. "Well, not to guys though, right?"

"No," he said slowly. "I think it depends on the guy."

His voice drew her eyes. She held his gaze as he spoke now.

"Some guys are too unsure, like you are now, and they're scared for the same reason. Others are just as desperate to be loved as you are and they make mistakes; loving the wrong person, getting hurt, and never loving again. And then, the kind

I think you need, is someone who will wait for you, love you, let you lead when you need to, and then take over before you ask. You also need someone to lift you up when you're down and not make you feel guilty about. I get the feeling you're down these days."

She stared, hypnotized. His mouth moved slowly as he spoke, and he glowed with a warm, radiant sun as he spoke. That light gleamed constant. He spoke honestly about a truth he believed in. Somehow, he had seen right through to her heart and read every desire there. She had no secrets from him. He read her like an exciting novel.

She had to remind herself to breathe as she stared into his eyes. *No more eye contact,* she chided herself.

She lifted her bags. "I think I'm done shopping. I have what I need."

"Let's do something else then." He put his arm around her shoulders and guided her away from the merchandise and the crowd that formed as the conferences ebbed and flowed. "There's a conservatory upstairs. Let's get some tea and just get away from people before we send you back in."

"Tea?" she joked. "Interesting."

"You are a coffee type, I take it?"

They went to the food court and got drinks from a small shop. Brigit knew it wouldn't be as good as Mary's coffee. Still, she was thankful for the diversion, even so early in the day.

"Well, I like teas because I like herbs," she said casually. "My mom liked the healing properties and all that. She knew what to use for calming, for stress, for headaches, even joint pain. She knew all the balms."

He held open the conservatory door for her. Surrounded by glass, the air moved through the oscillating fans clean and fresh with the scent of plants and flowers.

"I love flowers, she said.

He didn't reply. He watched her, and she tried not to notice. She touched a succulent and traced its stem. It soothed her to get away from the con crowd.

"You know, you remind me of how I used to be," she said finally, anxious at the silence he let play out. "Or rather, how I wanted to be. Actually, I wanted someone to make me be like that. Someone to show me the not so dark side of things, you know?"

He nodded, letting her talk.

"Normally, I'm too loud or pessimistic or too something for people. Now I'm just too depressed. I don't really think anyone would want to hang around me longer than they needed to." She sighed. "Sorry, this is me being open, I guess. I should stop."

"I don't think you're too anything, really." He still casually leaned on the wall near a bed exploding with fire-colored lilies. "Just human."

She tried to keep her eyes locked on his. She wanted to read what passed behind those kind, brown eyes, but couldn't find it.

"I better go, I guess. The panels I want to sit in on are about to start, plus I have a long drive home."

He nodded. "Maybe I'll see you around. Check out your store again."

She walked past him, not looking up at him to avoid distracting herself. "Yeah, I'll have some new stuff soon, I hope. Thanks for the coffee."

She caught his reflection in the glass door before pushing it open. She fought the urge to turn around and look into his mysterious face one last time. The reflection was almost too enticing.

Chapter 7

These Darker Streets

"That's not how I do business," Brigit sighed to an old woman with an armload of her merchandise.

"I will give you fifty dollars for the whole bunch. That's more than it's worth!" Spit flew from her mouth as she raged.

"I'm sorry, ma'am." She had no feelings of remorse, and it came through in her tone. She had to at least sound civil, to keep her head today. In just an hour, she would meet with her father to discuss the last details of the funeral. Then it would be over. Gone. "If you'd like, I do offer layaway on the more expensive things, like that altar blade."

"Fah!" The woman threw all the shiny and magic talismans onto the counter and stormed out, screaming a curse. The locals of the small town were always charming and understanding.

Mary dodged her in expert fashion on her way in. "The Ducati drove by again!" she giggled, handing Brigit a Chai. "That has to be the second time today. I've been watching."

"You're always watching people out of your little coffee window like a professional spy." She checked her phone again.

"What are you doing?" Mary asked when Brigit didn't look up for a second longer than she should have.

"I called my dad this morning to see if we were still on for the meeting." She put on her brave voice. The one she used when depression or anxiety got to her. She hoped no one else would notice.

"Did he say something to make you think otherwise?"

"No, I just wanted him to call, you know?"

"No." She shook her head and took a sip of coffee. "The man took your sister before your brother was even born and left you. He, what, calls on Christmas?"

Sometimes, she wanted to say. She couldn't bring herself to paint her father in a bad light. "I just want to give him a chance."

"Speaking of chances," Mary trilled. "Ducati at twelve o'clock. Again."

"Outside your store," Brigit smirked. "If you like him so much, who don't you ask him out?"

Mary put her cup down. "Brig, have I ever given you that 'I think you should try a man' speech?"

"What? No. Doesn't sound like one I need to hear."

"Okay, how about the 'what love can do for you' rant instead?"

"Mary, c'mon!"

"No, I'm serious, alright?" Her friend put her hand down on the counter like an angry teacher. "When I first met Jason, do you think I understood where I was? Or what he was? He was so messed up and into weird music and the paranormal, I couldn't handle him."

"In the throes of utter anarchy and perfect chaos, if I

remember what you said correctly." Brigit smiled, lessening the jibe in the words. "You've always believed in love and romance and magic."

"You did too!"

"When I was in college." Brigit made a stern face. "Life has taught me a lesson. All I can do is survive right now. Besides, Jason left you for that weird girl from the medieval festival, right?"

Mary winced, growling into her coffee cup. "Doesn't mean I don't know the good a companion can do for you."

Brigit checked her watch. "I have to go. Lock up for me? And don't forget Henry!"

She almost ran out of her own store. Mary opened her mouth to go on a rant about how love could heal the most mysterious wounds. How humans needed companionship - the most basic necessity of existence. About how magic can happen between any two people. She knew Mary would say all these things because she had before, and she didn't want to hear them again. Especially if it involved a guy who wore trinities on his belt buckle and long coats in public. And who had luscious, long, dark hair. And deep, wise, yet playful eyes. A guy who looked like a fighter, and had the laugh of a lover.

Nope, definitely not. Especially if it had to do with that.

The place she set up to meet her father was an old favorite of his that she had been avoiding for decades now. A multipurpose building with a great, golden theatre in the back that sometimes hosted dinner theaters. The front showed a bit more casual side, though. She liked it because it sported a Renaissance theme. When in college, she had done her under-graduate in Renaissance studies. She had loved the history that had to do with Old English, the Vikings, and all the other pieces that had come together to create the England she loved. And fairy tales were the best part. Imps, dryads, fairies, and kings - it used to give her chills.

She came fully prepared to go on, but reality struck, and she realized she needed to make money, so she switched to a major that would prepare her for owning a business. She had lucked into the place she (and before her, her mother) currently rented for her store and had done her best not to let it slip through her fingers. She had run the place successfully and satisfactorily. She had magic herbs, cauldrons, books on spells, and tons of fantasy reading. She had lamps that were dragons, talismans for every occasion, and even some things she wasn't sure what they were. People like her spent money on those. She felt like she cheated people.

The memories of her past life kept her distracted as she sipped on her second glass of wine near a huge reproduction of the statue of David by Michelangelo when she realized what she had known all along. He wasn't coming. Not now. Not then. Not later. He'd left her again. Everything rested on her. She had to bury her mother alone. She stared into the dregs of her wine-glass and willed herself not to cry. She couldn't cry; she had to get the job done. She had to face reality and acknowledge its governance in her life.

She sniffed. Tears were burning her eyes, threatening to spill out and let her secret strength go.

"No," she whispered. "You will suck it up. You have to. You

have to be strong just a bit longer." She met her own eyes in a mirror behind the greeter's stand. "Do you understand? It's just a bit."

A year ago, she would have gone to her store and read her own tarot to make herself feel better. She never put too much stock in tarot cards because she knew how to read them however she wanted. She always predicted the best fortunes for herself. Now she had no time, and certainly no energy, for frivolous hope in silly things.

She shoved herself away from the table and went to pay her bill. The young boy behind the register had to be only eighteen. He smiled and took her card.

"If you ever stand a girl up," she began, realizing tears were streaking down her face. The boy froze, handing her card back. "Men are rats. No, that's too simple. I don't know. Why don't I know?"

The wine put the words in her mouth. She drank too much. Couldn't she control herself just a little more? This wasn't her. She wasn't the moping type. Maybe a little, but not like this.

"Ugh." She got into her car and tried to find her phone to call Mary. She didn't want to drive all the way back to her apartment above the store. Mary lived closer, and she really shouldn't be driving.

"I hate when no one is here to rant to," she said to the ringer on Mary's phone as she pulled out of the parking lot. "Makes me feel crazy, talking to myself. Mary!" she shouted when the machine prompted her. "I need to crash at your place. I need to talk to you. To someone and you know you're the only someone who can put up with me when I'm like this. I'm a mess. I want to talk about mom. I need someone to help me with this funeral and I need..." she thought. "I need cream cheese and a bagel. Ugh, I should not be driving. Please call me."

She tossed her phone into the next seat and focused back on the road. *This is such a bad idea,* she thought. Should she be driving? She wanted to get away, so yes. The wine made her relax a little, bringing tears, which was always the worst. She had makeup in her eyes and it stung. She rubbed her eyes and pinched them closed.

Her car jerked to the right, and she screamed, over-correcting the wheel to the left. It had been drizzling, and her tire hit some water. She hydroplaned and spun out of control, her headlights flashed on trees and the open road as she spun once and then stopped, jerking as she hit a tree. Her head hit the wheel with a crack, and she saw a white light.

It only took a second, or so she thought, to shake the shock off. She got out and inspected the damage to her car. The headlight got bashed out, the fender crunched into the wheel well and caved into her tire, puncturing it. She couldn't drive.

"Wonderful!" she screamed into the woods. "Thanks. The store window and now the tire!"

In her backseat, she kept a nest of a year's worth of newspapers she'd stocked up on in case Henry had an accident outside his litter box. She rustled through about five before spotting a towing company in the ads. Only one nearby stayed open this late at night. A chipper voice answered, took her location, and said a truck would be out in just a few minutes and would she like to stay on the phone until the truck arrived.

"No, but thanks." How courteous.

She sat in her broken car and tried to wipe some of the stains off her face. Her tears were dry, but the tracks were bold.

She waited just a moment before the headlights appeared in her mirror, flashing yellow alerting her to its safe presence. She got out of her car and greeted the driver.

"Thanks for being the one place open." She tried to smile politely, wincing in the bright lights, the wine finally dissipated. She shielded her eyes, thinking she might be seeing things. A tall figure in a long coat stood before her. "Ildanach?" she gasped.

He inspected her car right away. "Glad you remember me. Looks like you did a pretty bang-up job, Brigit."

Her name rang sweetly in his voice.

He came back and stood beside her. For the first time, something like work, a crowd, or roller luggage full of art did not part them. She had no excuses. She finally took in how tall he was. Even though his hair lost its shine, damp from the rain, his eyes were still playful.

"I can give you a ride home if you'd like. I was going to grab some dinner if you're hungry."

She could see so clearly now. She realized she had ordered no food and became aware of her empty stomach, a small growl egging her on. His eyes were so intense. So hopeful. Why say no? Why say yes? Something inside her wouldn't let her refuse. An urgency built up in her stomach and clenched her heart. She had to breathe deeply to relieve the feeling.

"I know a place," she said at last.

Chapter 8

Mystery

"Do you come here a lot?" he asked, pulling a chair out for her. She hadn't said she did. He could just tell from the way she talked about the portraits, the architecture, and the piano on the stage in the back. "You seem to really know the place," he added when she looked up at him. He smiled, glancing down her bohemian blouse since he towered above her. She had smooth, pale breasts. He wondered if the rest of her looked like that. Smooth and calm, compared to her angry eyes and fiery hair.

"Why this place?" He sat opposite her and watched as she opened the menu. He could tell she felt tense. With her guard up, he couldn't see inside her. Being low on glow made his strength wane. Robin had given him a little vial of it. While her eyes scanned the menu, not moving much, he dumped the glow into the beer he ordered. After his first long draft, his senses kicked in and his powers heightened. He suddenly became aware of all the surrounding people, their life-force an ever-beating pulse. He even spotted some fairies among them.

"My father used to take me here," she said when he focused

on her again. She had put the menu down with elbows resting on the table. She relaxed a little. "Every Sunday. We had dinner and sometimes went to see the pianists if they had a good one. I loved it."

Ildanach didn't press the matter. She turned red when she mentioned her father. "You don't play?"

Her eyes finally met his. It came as a relief, as if she had been avoiding his gaze all night. When she had gotten into his truck, she had nearly gasped. He knew it was a nice truck, clean and full of high-tech equipment, but he had never paid it much mind. She had inspected the leather seats casually and sat down as though trying to hover over them. "It's nice," she had said. She hadn't expected him to have money and avoided his eyes the entire drive. Not now.

"Well, my father used to pay for lessons," she said. She turned so cute when she got tense. Her eyebrows twitched together. "When he really left, like stopped calling and sending birthday cards, I stopped playing. The magic had gone out of it, you know?"

He shook his head. "I've never been so affected by people. Did you not enjoy it?" He tried to see beyond her angst. She had a beautiful soul. If only she'd let him see it. He had to know.

"I liked it. But there's no real magic in music, right? It's all rhythms, beats per measure, and scientific. That's what father used to say."

Ildanach waved his hand quickly in front of her. "Enough about him. What made you quit?"

She held his gaze again. He looked deep. Igniting the glow inside, he thrust himself past her eyes to see her aura. There it was. The fire that only Brigit had, burning from thousands of years ago. The raging passion, the love, the memories. Everything that made his wife from an age past rested there, locked in her mind.

He got just a glimpse before she shut him out.

"What are you staring at?" she snapped.

He motioned to the passing waiter for the check. "What are you so suspicious of?" he asked, sliding a large pile of bills to the end of the table, his eyes never leaving hers. "I've never met someone so guarded."

She didn't waver, tap her fingers, or look away. Her confidence in what she would say was steadfast. "I'm not. I'm angry, I'll admit it. However, that's no one's business. Mary says I should let it out." She shook her head. "There's no place in this world for that."

Smiling, he leaned across the table. "You know the clearing in Oakvale Nature Preserve?"

Confused, she nodded. "The one right off the highway. Where they built that overpass."

"Yeah," he said sadly. "Can I show you something there?"

"Now?" Brigit cried, laughing humorlessly. When he kept smiling hopefully, she sighed and texted Mary that she was going to the preserve. To Ildanach, she said, "If I'm not back in town in twenty minutes, you're dead. Trust me."

"I appreciate your candor." Grinning boyishly, he led her to the truck.

They drove for only a few minutes, going beyond the little city into the nature preserve just outside of town. He took her hand and walked past the ranger outpost to the opening behind it. At first her hand lay limp in his, but soon he felt her fingers clasp around his. She decided to willingly follow, no doubt curious. For now, anyway. He had to calm the fire in his heart.

"Listen here," he whispered. They were just outside the border of the trees. "Inside this forest is a clearing. Long ago, the people who founded this village believed in a kind of magic. Music was part of that. They would play pipes and sing and dance here to remember their ancestors and praise the powerful deities beyond the veil."

He felt rather than saw Brigit shift her weight. "Is this about magic?"

"Some people from this little town in Ohio are descendants of great Celtic magic workers, Brigit. Their magic remains. Don't you have any faith in anything? Magic comes in all shapes and forms."

He turned her to him and took her shoulders in his strong hands. She seemed so small and lost. She gazed up at him, asking him to explain, afraid of the answer. Her arms wrapped around herself. How could she say no and get him to understand so he didn't leave?

"I have hopes and dreams, sure." She shrugged, both hating and loving his hands on her shoulders. "I want my business to grow. I want to teach classes on meditation and health, like Mary keeps bugging me to do. And I could, if I would just do it. I have bigger businesses offering me positions in their marketing departments because they knew my father and think my resume is nice and shiny. I have options."

"What's stopping you?" His voice became soft. "If you're so confident?"

Her heart fell a little. She didn't know. And she didn't actually have confidence in her abilities. "Isn't there more out there?" she said quietly, afraid to say the wrong thing. "More than owning a business or making someone else look good? I mean, you seem pretty mysterious and well off. How do you do it with a junkyard?"

She began shivering. He took his long coat off and pulled her close, draping it over her shoulders. She looked minuscule in it.

"Your confusion and anger are refreshing. People who seem to have it all together are boring, and they bother me. I feel like they're not looking deep enough. How can you be satisfied in a world such as this?" He waved his hand across the dark horizon where the stars kissed the earth.

He couldn't push her. Not now. He knew that. Suddenly, he wanted her and just her. Not the woman he knew from thousands of years ago. Not the woman he tricked himself into thinking Jennifer might be. He had mourned that loss, and now he found the real thing. She wasn't that other Brigit from a hundred years ago he loved now. This one from the twenty-first century with her Chai and her angry driving made his heartbeat. Her fear and fearlessness. Her anger and her hidden joy. This was the one.

She clutched the fronts of his coat where it hung on her shoulders. He smiled into the night. A warmth radiated in her chest at his smile. He relaxed when he caught the tension leave her just a little. Her heart pounded so loudly it was the only thing he could hear in the darkness. He swore he saw steam rising from her now, not just her breath.

"I try to be satisfied," she said. "And Mary would say that men like women of confidence. No mystery needed." She giggled nervously. Catching herself, she gritted her teeth to stop from chattering. It wasn't the cold that made her shake now. She was almost sweating into his coat.

Ildanach shrugged in his charming way. "I like some mystery."

He looked right at her when she turned to face him.

"You don't think I'm going too crazy over this...this..." she didn't want to use the word funeral just now. "I am though. I'm an angry mess."

His hands went right to her face, cupping it gently. "Feeling all these emotions is the best part of being a living thing. Don't feel guilty about your life because someone you love has lost theirs."

"They didn't lose it, it was taken," she sobbed quietly. "No one understands what's going on." She hiccuped into utter defeat. "Mary tries to be supportive, often trailing off to other topics when I try to release my feelings. There's almost no one else I can turn to for a solid rock to hold on to."

Ildanach lifted her face again, this time with the one hand. With the other, he wiped her tears away and pushed her hair back behind one ear.

"No one will ever get you all the time. But someone will always be there for you. You don't have to fight alone."

S he reached up and put her hands over his, his skin warm in the night air. His hands were strong and suddenly she wanted nothing more than to be lifted up by him and carried in his arms, wrapped in his coat. She inhaled and took in his scent, committing it to memory: fire and the sweet smell of dusty books all at once, strength and kindness and a fierce loyalty.

Her heart quickening, she licked her lips and looked up into his dark eyes. A fierceness sparked there she hadn't seen before. Like a wild boar hunter waiting to pounce. It drew her in and made a hot pulsing between her legs she had ignored for far too long. He waited for her to move. That's all it would have taken; just a little lean in and a small amount of willingness. A piece of her could heal.

"Can you take me home?" she said softly, lowering her eyes at last. There. She forced the moment to be over. Gone.

He said nothing the entire drive back, and walked her to her door.

"I'll call you when the parts come in," he said.

She stopped before walking up the stairs to her home above her shop. "And I'll order that talisman for you." She couldn't look back. She had to stay strong. "I'll see you later, then," she said.

Chapter 9

Is It Wrong?

The night before hung in Brigit's mind like a smelly dish rag. She wanted to ignore it, tell herself she could have behaved worse. It kept creeping back into her mind. Maybe not as unpleasant as a dish rag's smell, but it made her wince. Plus, now was not the time to worry about a man. Not even close.

She tried not to scrutinize herself too much while the black blob of mourning stared back at her with a glassy gaze from the mirror. Today, she buried her sorrows. And her family. She hadn't bothered to call her father and didn't even know her sister's phone number. If they wanted to, they'd be there. She decided what she'd say to them if they did arrive, black-clad like her and mourning. Would they mourn? Or would they just show up so the papers wouldn't say how one of the greatest CEOs of the city hadn't even shown up at his ex-wife's funeral. And if he came, it would just be to harass her about taking a job inside his company. He hated her store. Always had. Wished she'd done something bigger with her talent. She thought about painting the top so he could see it from his top floor at the end of the main street. These thoughts pushed

Ildanach out of her head and replaced them with things to say to people who came to honor her mother and brother. She had to say something. People had been sending cards, flowers, and leaving wonderful brief messages on her phone all day. She owed them something.

She came down from the loft and looked around for Henry. He had to be cooped up all day as Mary said she'd host the gathering after the funeral at her house. She'd let the little guy run around for a few hours. She passed the front door and realized a package waited for her outside. Making sure Henry wouldn't dash out the door, she opened it and picked up the little box. Inside, the special amulet Ildanach liked and asked her to order rested among packing peanuts.

It was small and made of pewter. He had been insistent that she not order the copper or iron one. She had said that either of those were far more unique than the plain pewter, but he insisted. The highly intricate design had intertwined bands, and each one of those had runes meticulously carved into them. No larger than her palm, she couldn't even count all the many runes.

She weighed it in her hand. It felt solid. Supposedly designed to protect against evil spirits and feelings of loss, she tied a leather cord around it and slung it over her head. Why not take it for a test drive? Besides, she'd like to see him wear it knowing she had too. She kissed it and tucked it down her shirt. The cold against her cleavage made her gasp before her body heated it quickly.

Now, to the job at hand. She found Henry napping in the Druid cloaks folded under a table and put him away just when Mary arrived to drive her to the church.

"Ready?" Mary asked quietly. It made Brigit conscious of her grief all over again.

"Yeah." Brigit surprised herself with the word. She put her hand over the amulet. "When we get back to your place, can we talk? I'd like to run something by you."

"Of course." Ever the best friend. Brigit tried to relax, grateful.

The service ran short and meaningful. Brigit had arranged for only those closest to her mother and brother to show up and thanked any listening deity that the line of people filing in to nod sympathetically was short. Everyone who gave her their condolences just made her heart heavier with every story they told.

"I never met you," one boy with tasseled blonde hair said to her. "I recognize you from Jay's pictures. I'm Gabe; I was his roommate. He thought you were pretty cool. Said you raised him after his dad left and stuff."

In the teenager's eyes, she saw his hurt as well. He worked up his courage to be brave and not show emotion, to cover his quivering voice. "He was a great guy, though. Could do awesome things on a skateboard."

Brigit laughed here, nodding through her heartache. "He was so brave on that thing. Reckless and crazy too."

"Yeah, he told me about the time you drove him to get stitches after he wiped out on a rail. Said not to tell your mom." The boy smiled. His genuine love spread to her.

She smiled too. "Yeah. He scared the crap out of me. He comforted *me* the whole time. I only had my learner's permit and shouldn't have been driving. I should have..." She stopped. "It was nice to meet you, Gabe."

Brigit glanced around to see if her father had shown up. Not so much as a limo pulled up.

It went for just a few more minutes. When everyone had finally trickled out, taking their mandatory remarks with them, Mary walked with Brigit to the car and drove to her house, where they hid in the back room so Brigit could talk.

"I've been over this funeral thing for weeks now," she started. "I tried to get my father to come and show some respect, but no. I'm fed up with him and all of this." She motioned to her black clothes.

"Where are you going with this?" Mary asked, a little on edge.

"I know there is no such thing as true love," Brigit went on. She raised her hand to silence Mary, who inhaled sharply to protest. If anyone believed in love, Mary did. "I know life just sucks because it does. What if I tried to find a little happiness? Is it wrong that I want that so soon after, you know..."

Mary's eyes popped. "No!" she almost shouted. "Brig, holy Ra, are you kidding me? Wanting to be happy is not wrong. Ever." She waited for that to sink in. Brigit had something in mind. "What is it?"

"I'm *not* seeing a guy," Brigit laid emphasis on the word. "I may have been thinking about that guy Ildanach, though. Or is that wrong?" she questioned quickly.

Mary giggled into her hand.

"I mean, he's so weird and a little out there. And did you know he's got money too? Somehow his little business is turning a profit. Maybe he's a front for the mob..."

"Or family money," Mary smiled, rubbing her finger and thumb together, wiggling her brows as she did.

"Stop!" Brigit swatted at her friend, a laugh rattling in her grief-worn chest. "Last night he was just so...amazing."

"Last night!" Mary gasped. "Amazing? Was that the text you sent me? Tell me everything!"

"Ugh, no, we didn't do anything. We went to look at the woods and talk."

"The woods, huh? Is that your code word?" She winked.

Brigit blushed deeply. She had sat up all night wondering if she let an excellent opportunity to relieve some stress go by. Then again, she wasn't that type of girl. She had one-night stands before and didn't like it. That probably helped her decide to swear off men and focus on her career. That and her father didn't give men a very good image.

"I just want to know if it would be wrong of me to try again," she said at last.

"No," Mary cooed. "I can't believe it. I thought you'd die an old spinster with a hundred ferrets, all alone."

"Thanks." She had a point. Brigit didn't believe in love. Love, romance, and magic made fairy tales and movies. No guy wanted commitment anymore. No guy could be loyal. No guy would come to his ex-wife and son's funeral. She hadn't wanted a relationship. Not in a long time. But something about Ildanach told her it might work. He could be different.

He laughed a lot and smiled. He wasn't all dark and broody or carrying around a need to be a harsh man with a loud voice, always talking about his achievements. He had strength, though. His greatest strength came in a kind of silence he didn't need to boast about. She could see his strength in his arms and hands. She loved his hands, the way they had felt on hers. She longed to be touched by his hands again, just to see what it felt like.

She wondered what the rest of him looked like.

"No, no, no!" Brigit leapt up and frantically paced the room. "What am I thinking? I can't just up and go out with a guy."

"Huh?" Mary looked just as shocked as Brigit felt agitated. "Yes, you can. How else does one do it? Stop being a nun!"

"But...but..." she stuttered. She couldn't think of a reason not to. Why did she have to be this way? Why did she have to be afraid of anything she couldn't explain? Love was the worst. She tried to tell herself she just lusted after this guy. Yeah, that's all she wanted; just a fling to get herself back on track. Could it be as simple as that? If she wanted to be with him—in any capacity —she had to take a chance if she ever wanted to feel normal again.

"Alright." She clasped the amulet. "I guess I'll give it a try."

Chapter 10

On The Hunt

Ildanach stared into the shimmering liquid he currently consumed from a round, glass bottle. Glow was steadily fading into a precious commodity he had heard and now he had to go find out why. Without it, his powers would dwindle and become weak. Would it kill him? No, he'd live forever. That had been established during the awful war in the years prior. Glow faded into scarcity more than than it did now. They engaged in a civil war in their world over whether or not to help the humans. Their language changed and so had their religion. He took a wound in the war and had not died then. Fairies never died.

The glow reminded him of her eyes. It glittered a kind of purple that changed to green in the sunlight and glinted with a hidden passion. If only he had been more forceful. More urgent, perhaps. His body cried out to be touched by her once again. Stronger still was the way his heart ached. It beat for her and only her all these years. He wondered if his true love would ever walk this earth again, or if he was doomed to eternity without her. Now she appeared, magically coming into his life.

"Pondering great, deep, guardian things?" Robin asked, coming in from the yard. "Hunting soon? You only drink that much when you're going out."

Ildanach raised one eyebrow and shrugged. "I was going to find others and see if I can trace this lack of glow. It doesn't make sense why it's getting so scarce."

Robin folded his arms on the table and set his chin down in the crook of his elbow. His eyes lingered on the glow. "Unlike humans, the fairies can't be tricked into giving more away. I suppose I could go back behind the veil and get some myself."

"You?" Ildanach laughed. "Aren't you still on probation from our world? Something about turning a human into an ass."

Robin rolled his eyes. "All humans are asses at one point or another. What was the big deal? Besides, that was a long, *long* time ago!"

"The big deal was that you made the fairy queen into an ass as well." He smiled.

"I was under orders!" Robin used his old excuse casually. "So, what are you going to do with next to no glow? If you get weak, as the guardian, who knows what could happen. The poor silly humans wouldn't be safe."

No, none of them would be safe. He only cared about Brigit. If only he didn't have to love her and lose her every lifetime. It got harder and harder every time.

"There is only one human you care about," Robin said, prompting Ildanach to finally tell him the story. The goblin had been harassing him for years to know why he did the job of guardian for so long. "Why do you not let the torch pass to another fairy? If you step down, another guardian can take your place. It's happened before."

Ildanach reached to his belt and placed his magic sling onto the table. "This was a gift from my adopted father. The fairies blessed it and can kill dark spirits. It was given to me. Not anyone else." He frowned. "Who would even want this life?"

"Killing dark spirits, chasing hellhounds, hunting down gargoyles and werewolves! Yeah, I'd take it." Robin looked up at him with bright eyes, fascinated by the life he imagined Ildanach lived.

"Living ostracized from your world. Finding the one woman you love again and again, same soul, different body, only to lose her after falling for her every time. Do you know how many times I have watched my love die? Her blood on my hands and my face. Her screams echoing in my ears and her eyes, eternally petrified and frightened, looking to me to save her...and I can't!"

Ildanach stood up and slammed his hands on the table. The bottle of glow rattled but didn't fall over. He snatched it up. He was losing control of himself. Getting too emotional. "I have to go. Arawn is out there somewhere and needs to be watched. Don't wait up for me."

The setting sun blinded him every other block as it flashed between buildings. He drove for an hour and had not seen so much as the dust of a pixie. Ready to give up after a few hours, he spotted an old man with a dog on a street corner. The dog, just a Great Dane to the eyes of the humans, watched a boy across the street, its ears down and nose forward. He recognized the old man as well: Arawn's favorite disguise. The old man watched the boy, mumbling something to the hound, preparing to reap a soul.

Ildanach looked around. The tiny town normally closed up around five, so the streets were relatively clear. Still, it was his job to keep them and the fairies on this side of the veil safe. He couldn't charge in now.

But he had to save the boy. Gritting his teeth, Ildanach revved his engine and charged toward the hound. It could look like an accident if he got out quick. Sometimes, his job turned gruesome and grim.

The Ducati picked up speed in the few yards it took to catch up to the corner where Arawn stood plotting his reaping. Hearing the bike, he whirled around just in time to leap out of Ildanach's way. The hound didn't come out so fortunate, though. He hit the hell beast square in the side, forcing a pained yelp. It took just three seconds for Ildanach to unsheathe his iron blade with the leather handle, stab the hound, and rev his bike out of the street, never leaving the seat. He knew the people would be dumbfounded, and that Arawn would be right on his tail. He wouldn't mourn the loss of his hound; he'd attack.

Behind him, he heard a chorus of howls and the rumbling of Arawn's own huge, red Harley. All the fairies had a pension for fast vehicles these days and the darker spirits were no exception.

Ildanach led his pursuer out of town and into an abandoned factory where they could do battle outside of the human's gaze. Ildanach hadn't anticipated just how big the wolf pack was. He ramped up an old drop off plank and landed inside the decaying building with a plethora of rainbow words and images graffitied on the walls.

He turned his bike sharply, coming to a screeching halt only to jump when the growls of hounds already at the factory alerted him to the danger behind. There were three and who knows how many more coming with Arawn. He kicked the floor and swiveled his bike around to go back out the way he'd come, hopefully leaving the hounds behind. There, in the doorway, Arawn waited, his wide hat still somehow on his head after the chase.

"Time to give up, Ildanach," he said in a deep voice. "The pack have you surrounded."

"How can you think that a few mutts will stand a chance against me when I've outrun such things for thousands of years?" He tried to sneer even though he couldn't find anything funny about it. He had to think fast. Fortunately, he had a lot of glow flowing inside him.

"Cocky bastard." Arawn's voice rumbled.

The hounds barked sharply and charged Ildanach. He had just long enough to unsheathe his iron blade again before two hounds were on him, teeth snapping and claws raking at his face. He had forgotten what it felt like to be hurt. The pain of his flesh being torn created a sensation he had not missed feeling.

He got the blade into one hound, its hot, molten blood burning through his leather-clad arms, missing his gloves. He cried out as a second wolf pounced, knocking him off his ride at last. The bike fell over, trapping his leg underneath with two massive dogs on top, glaring down at him. They were not hiding any more. The real beasts looked down at him, licking their black teeth and squinting with eyes of fire. Their charred flesh oozed from the constant ring of fire that burned just over their skin. They all bore numerous scars that knotted and disfigured their skin.

"Fetch," Arawn ordered.

Two hounds chomped his wrists between their maws and dragged him out from under the bike. The pain cracked through his leg as they tugged. He held his lips tightly shut so Arawn wouldn't know of his pain.

The dark spirit reached down and took the blade from Ildanach's shaking hand. The hound's teeth buried deep into his flesh. "I've always wondered how you carried these," Arawn said. "I see. Leather made from a black stag. Very special leather. Blocks all the power of iron." He flipped it around in his hand. "Is this the one you stabbed me with?"

Ildanach only struggled once before realizing it brought greater pain. His leg throbbed from the fall, and he could feel his blood leaking from his gashed wrists. He felt a little faint. He had to hold on.

"Why are you hesitating?" he asked. His voice shook, but he made it into a growl. "I'm sure my soul would look great in your collection."

"Ildanach, my boy, I've been around a lot longer than you have." He held the blade pointed down and knelt next to his captive. He placed the tip in the center of his neck, where it sizzled softly. "I've always had this one job. Take souls when they are ready. It's so easy. Do you know what it's like to rip a live, pulsing soul from a mortal body? Near impossible. I reach in, grasp the little thing, and my hounds tear into the mortal's flesh. It's easier when they're almost dead. Still the soul resists.

The skin peels from my hands as I pull, my fingernails burn away, and I bleed. It's not pleasant."

Ildanach shook his head. "So, why do that? Are you not satisfied with taking the many that are ready to leave?"

"It's not that; it never is." With a strong, wide stroke, he slashed Ildanach's chest with the blade, drawing dark purple blood.

Ildanach screamed from the sudden pain, quickly closing his mouth and squeezing his eyes, willing the tears to not fall to show weakness.

"I make them despair first. Like a good old-fashioned haunting." Arawn went on. He stood up and sauntered back to his bike, letting his hounds gnash their teeth into Ildanach's bloodied flesh. "It is so much easier to take a soul that way. Step one is infestation: I follow them, put thoughts into their head, shroud their will, frighten them. Step two: I press them, create despair. Step three: obsession with their misery. Then..." He made a swiping motion with the blade. "Too easy. So much more enjoyable."

Ildanach heard enough to understand. He needed to tell Robin so he could alert the other fairies. To protect the mortals. Arawn had started a reaping rampage, taking souls before their time. Not only did this disrupt the balance of one life enters while another leaves, but it was also cruel.

With a deep roar, he swung his long, muscled legs around and knocked the hounds away from him. In that one second of surprise, he got the moment he needed to run back to his bike, using the last of the glow inside of him to dull the pain in his legs, heal a little, and charge out the door. To his surprise, Arawn didn't follow him. He knew this meant they were not through. The dark spirit had more planned than he had shared. Ildanach didn't have time to hear it. A threat from a powerful rogue spirit endangered the world he protected. He wanted to go to Brigit and make sure she was safe. She wouldn't listen to him now. And he couldn't show up, chewed on, bloody and broken. No, he had to wait for the right moment to tell her everything.

Chapter 11

Deeper Into Darkness

Brigit eyed her phone for the millionth time that day. She counted ten times before lunch and then twenty-five since then. Almost four in the evening. Surely Ildanach would close up shop soon. She hadn't heard from him at all the day before, and he said he'd call her when her car was fixed. Or should she call him to say his order came in? Yeah, that would be fine. After all, that's what normal owners did when orders came in for clients, right? She picked up her phone. The number for his junkyard and shop still the first one in her phone's memory. Redial just required the press of one button. So easy to push.

A group of kids entered her store, looking for goat-head pentagrams. She told them sorry, she didn't have those. They wanted to know why not, and she just shrugged. Apparently, those meant magic to kids these days. She didn't know the half of it, but was certain it had nothing to do with the Celtic lore she promoted. After a small back and forth, she realized they were just edgy teens looking for a token to flaunt.

These days, she didn't even know what qualified as magic. That was more Mary's department now. "But you bought me my first fantasy novel!" Mary would say whenever Brigit laughed off magic and romance. She wasn't sure when that part of her life had vanished. She held onto the store for her mother: a hard-core follower of the old ways, as she put it. Ildanach seemed to know a thing or two about it. Maybe she could ask him. Yeah, just to chat. When she picked up her car. There might be a lot to talk about, though. They'd probably have to go out to discuss things properly. Maybe he could remind her what it felt like to dream, imagine, and believe in something beyond this world's explanations.

"Scaredy-cat, just call!" she growled. Determined, she snapped up her phone and shushed the kids in the back by the incense. She hit redial. It rang. Her heart pounded like she had just run a marathon. Not that she'd ever run one—she guessed it might feel like that. Her legs even tingled.

"Hi, thanks for calling Nocturne Automotive," a peppy voice chirped into her ear. "How can I assist you today?"

"Um," she mumbled. She had to get a grip. She had more strength than this. "I was wondering if Ildanach was in today? He's working on my car," she added quickly.

A moment of silence passed before the chirpy voice said, "Is this Brigit from the Celtic store?"

"Yeah, it's me. I just need my car, you know?" She bit her nails. She hadn't done that since before the funeral.

"Who is it?" said a hoarse voice from beyond the phone. It sounded like Ildanach, but deeper, strained. Even painful. Panic flitted through her chest. What was wrong with him?

"Ildanach, gods be damned, get back to bed!" the peppy one hissed.

Shuffling and snapping sounds told her the phone got forced away from the assistant. "Brigit?" He suddenly sounded a lot better. "I was going to call you and let you know I ordered the parts for your car. Should be here soon. I pulled some from another body shop."

Good, he had started the work for her. "Awesome! Also, your talismans came in and I thought I'd deliver it, so you didn't have to drive back in to town."

"Actually," a smile touched his voice. It made her own lips spread in a grin just to hear it. "I was thinking, you know that spot I showed you the other day? The local gathering is there tonight as it is All Hallows Eve. I was wondering if you wanted to go? It's small and no pressure, so..."

Her jaw dropped just a little in surprise. She had to hold her breath to make sure she didn't make any squeaky, excited noises. It seemed a little too convenient, right? A gathering on All Hallows Eve?

"Um, I don't know." She tried to sound aloof. "I've never been to that kind of thing. I didn't even know we had one." It was Ohio though; they loved that kind of thing. How could she not know? Had she really not been paying attention to life that much?

Ildanach laughed hoarsely. "Like I said, it's laid back. And I know for a fact that you have some great clothes in that store that would be perfect for it."

She glanced around. She'd never thought of wearing any of it. That belonged to a different crowd. Did he want her to? She wanted to give him a shot, right?

"Well, I can come up with something. It's not supposed to be too cold tonight."

He laughed, and it made her toes curl in excitement as something below her stomach tingled.

"Surprise me," he said softly. "I'll pick you up at eight, okay?"

Pick her up! "Alright," she said, holding in her excitement. "I'll do my best."

She turned to Henry, who looked at her with his liquid, knowing eyes. "Silly girl," he seemed to be saying from his hammock. "Don't you see how in love with him you are already?"

"Tch," she hissed. "There is no way I'm in love with him. I'm just excited to be going out. I haven't been out in years. Don't tell anyone, Henry!"

He yawned at her.

"I feel kind of weird, too. I'm not sure what he expects." She went to the store's rack and looked at the dresses she had consistently ordered for the last several years. Some were very thin, so she marked those out right away. Should she wear a costume? She knew some women who bought these just to wear in every day life. Those women were weird, right? Were these normal to him?

"I hate this stuff," she sighed, taking a dark green one embroidered with black triskelions, trinities, and looping vines. She'd try something silly for a chance with that guy. His charming, dark eyes. His luscious, long hair. His strong, fiery skin pressed up against hers.

She put the dress on, careful to pad her bra to hide any excitement she couldn't control or the cold, and chose a long, black coat with a pointed hood on it. That seemed appropriate, but she really had no idea. After that, she clasped a silver necklace with a magic symbol on it around her neck. Looking in the mirror, she hardly recognized herself. She looked like a priestess of Avalon or a long-lost queen.

Before she knew it, Ildanach appeared at her door, tapping on the glass. She let him in and noticed he still wore his black clothes, his long coat and hat.

"I guess you're always dressed for the occasion," she sighed. She balled her fist. "What do you think?" Last time they had been together—at the con—she had refused to do dress up. Now embarrassment ate at her cheeks, standing in this stupid dress and cloak.

His dark eyes roamed her up and down, lingering a little too long on her newly exposed cleavage. The sleeveless dress had a plunging neckline.

"You look like a vision," he whispered. He held out his hand, and she placed hers in his palm. He drew her hand to his lips, inhaled, and kissed her knuckles. She felt his teeth graze her flesh as he kissed her, his eyes never leaving hers. "You smell like frankincense."

She nodded, her face pulsing red. "I always smell. I mean, I sell oils." Her face would surely explode with tension.

He led her out and opened the door for her, his truck already warm inside from the heated seats. When he got in, the streetlight illuminated his arm as he reached up for the wheel.

All around his wrists were scars she had never noticed before. They looked like they had once been deep.

"Scars," she pointed. "I never noticed before."

He arched an eyebrow at her and glanced over with a playful smile. "I save them for when I need to convince girls how tough I am."

She saw right through his adorable facade. As though she had seen him lie a million times before and knew how to read it. She wanted to insist on knowing how he got them. She also didn't want to ruin the night before it even began. She kept her mouth closed.

The short drive soon saw them parked in the nature preserve's grassy lot, following a small stream of oddly-clad individuals into the woods. The path glowed, lined with candles, and off in the trees, near little bonfires, musicians played on flutes and drums.

"This is incredible," she breathed. She recognized some of her own merchandise on a few people and they waved to her, clearly knowing her. "I feel awful. All these people know me. I have no idea who they are."

He laughed. "Here, this is what I wanted to show you."

They appeared in a small clearing where the majority of the celebrators danced around a fire to drums and drinking out of goblets.

"This is weird, Ildanach," she said when they made it to the middle of the crowd. She shrunk into his side, trying to avoid passersby from touching her. "I mean, it's cool, but I have no idea..." She had no idea what to say is what she meant, even if the words wouldn't come. Especially since it felt so familiar. As if she had done this exact thing millions of times.

Ildanach stopped and faced her, pulling her under the shadow of a great oak tree. "Brigit, I'd like you to try something for me." His voice deepened to a serious tone. It was very sexy. She had to look into his eyes, no matter how intimidating it felt.

"Okay. What?"

He seemed so urgent. He licked his lips and glanced around. "Forget about everything tonight. Forget about the shop. About how hurt you are. About everyone here. No one is here. Just you."

"What are you talking about?" She swept her hand outward. "There are dozens of people here. And a lot of them know me."

He gently and urgently put his palms over her cheeks, cupping her face. "Brigit, my fiery phoenix, try. Please."

His face came suddenly so close to hers. What was going on? Her legs felt numb, her mind spinning, and all she could think of was Ildanach there before her. His brow cast a deep shadow over his face. It created a sort of darkness there that she had not seen before. Something old.

"Alright," she gasped after holding her breath. She had no idea what possessed her, making her pull back and hold herself up high.

Counting the drumbeats in her head, she began to pulse on her heels to feel it. The grass under her feet tickled. familiar and welcoming. The firelight suddenly didn't seem strange and scary, rather warm and friendly, as though she'd seen it all before.

Brigit removed her coat and raised her arms, swaying gently at first, still a little nervous. She watched the people around her. No one watched her. She let her hips lead then, swaying to the right and then her torso followed, her arms like water trailing behind. She didn't know she could move like that! Then she swayed the other way and felt a wonderful sensation inside her. The music came from inside her, dictating her steps, and she let it carry her.

She swayed in wider circles and turned, dramatically throwing her arms up into the air. Her eyes fell on Ildanach and she realized he had been watching her. She froze, her arms still up, and she suddenly felt foolish. She didn't have a moment longer to think about it. He smiled broadly and stepped closer, his arm encircling her waist, spinning her easily. She nearly tripped, but he scooped her up into his arms and spun her around, smiling charmingly into the night.

When he set her down, her courage returned, and she thrust her hips to the drums, her arms wiggling out to the side. His eyes were ever on hers, nowhere else, thirsty for her vision. The smile faded away, replaced by a fiery gaze full of yearning. His eyes became intense as he moved for her again, this time like a hunter. He took her hand and spun her around this way, then that. Out of her own control, she had to go where he led her. At first, she stumbled through it, then realized he wouldn't make her do anything she didn't want. She gave herself up to him like she'd done a million times before.

Have I? she suddenly thought.

He pressed himself up behind her, putting his hand on her collarbone, gently forcing her head back onto his shoulder. He swayed her in this way for a moment, letting his hand trail up her neck and onto her face. She found her own hands roaming behind, grasping his hard chest and abs. His other hand found her stomach and followed her curves to her hips. He squeezed her there, then let his hand fall lower, brushing her thighs and curving inward.

She gasped and threw her head back, her mouth hanging open for air. She reached back as they swayed; the drums pulsated around them. She grabbed his long hair in her fist. She leaned to the side, unconsciously making way for the first kiss he ever gave her. His lips were hot and supple on her neck as he kissed her lightly at first. Then the urgency grew, and his teeth nicked her flesh.

She threw herself around, facing him, and kissed his neck in return, hungry for his touch. He let her kiss him just twice before he took her face in his hands, stronger than before, and pushed his lips to hers. She inhaled his scent immediately, breathing him in and drinking up his kisses. He bit her lip and when she did not recoil, slid his tongue into her mouth, exploring her gently.

She arched into him, pushing her hips against him. She suddenly could not be close enough to him. She pulled him tightly against her, her arousal matching his; this encouraged her. She tried to take more of him in, locked at the lips as they were. The desire grew, overcoming her.

With an animal grunt, he broke away, pulling her into the darker shadows of the dense forest. He tugged her arm and resumed where he had stopped before hiding. His hands went from her shoulders to her breasts. Surprisingly, she didn't mind. Her hands roamed all over his hard chest, up and down to his belt buckle. They collapsed together and he rolled over on top of her, his hands roving down between her thighs. She spread her legs to ease his effort and started to work the buckles on his shirt. She needed him there. She hadn't felt this on fire in years.

He paused and she waited as they locked eyes. All the boyishness evaporated from his face. All the fear from hers. He transformed into a dark hunter and she the willing prey.

"Why are you stopping?" she panted. Her skirts were pulled up and his shirt hung open. The spot between her legs screamed.

"I don't feel like we should." His voice came strained and gruff. "Not yet."

Quite suddenly, she didn't either. Had she done something to upset him? What did she do wrong? She had moved too fast. He seemed to be able to read the panic and hurt on her face because he quickly kissed her again.

"It's not you, I swear." He stood and helped her up, sliding his coat back over her shoulders as she shivered. The heat had gone.

She tried to understand, but she just couldn't. "What is it? Please, tell me."

Regret mixed with longing darkened his handsome brow. "I will, one day soon. I swear."

"What's wrong with right now?" she asked. A lump formed in her throat. This wasn't fair at all.

"Please, Brigit." He reached up and wiped a tear she hadn't known trickled down her cheek. He tried to be so tender, but it still hurt. "I swear it will happen soon."

What else could she say? "Did I do something wrong?"

"No," he laughed, relieved it seemed. He kissed her on the lips once again, sweetly this time. "You are perfect. Wonderful and beautiful."

Her heart lifted, even if it still stung. "I don't understand is all."

"You will though, my love." He pulled her gently to him, allowing her to decide whether or not to come in. She let herself be guided back to him and his strong arms wrapped around her close. She could hear his heart beating, and it calmed her.

She sighed heavily. This, right here in his arms, surrounded by the woods and firelight, was where she wanted to be forever. If only such a thing as true love and forever existed.

Chapter 12

Earth Glows

"And breathe into your joints, raising your arms up, say thanks for today, and exhale down," the yoga instructor said in her deep, dreamy voice. Mary had finally convinced Brigit to try a class with her.

"This is a strong step," Mary whispered to Brigit, whose face turned red with effort. "Maybe it will inspire you to finally take my offer."

"I hate yoga," Brigit grunted through a rather strained upward-facing dog pose. "All that inner peace, strength, and believe in yourself shit."

"I doubt Krishna is blessing me right now as I sweat to his praises." She nodded in the direction of the stereo where soft, soothing chants flitted up to the ceiling, filling the room with soft bells and gentle voices.

"This is a good step," Mary insisted again. "You've really changed over the last few days. I think you're doing well. This will help you psychologically too."

"I'm not a mental patient, Mar, thanks." She heaved herself

up into a warrior pose. "Finally, my head above my ass." She panted. She caught sight of herself in the studio mirror. She looked pretty cool in this pose. Very strong and confident. Powerful even. She smiled at herself despite her red face and frizzy hair.

"I see that," Mary giggled. "So, this guy." She wiggled her eyebrows again when Brigit hissed at her to leave it alone. "Have you doinked him yet?"

Brigit wrinkled her nose this time. "Rhiannon Mary O'Shea, I'm not doinking a guy who believes in fairies. I'm just not." She ended on a strong note.

"Whoa, what are you full-naming me for?" Mary smirked and shook her head. "Why do you have to use the word doinking?" she asked, instead of pushing the topic.

"*You* said it!" Brigit growled in defense. The teacher glanced back at them, putting her finger to her lips for silence.

"Because he's so doinkable!" Mary said in a high-pitched voice she tried to keep quiet. She smiled, showing her white teeth in glee. "I mean, look at those huge, brown eyes! His hair. His style." She closed her eyes and moaned like a woman about to climax. "I have been thinking about what his body must look like ever since he first walked in."

So had Brigit, but she didn't want to say that. Not with so many people around. And she had had a chance to find out. She had seen his smooth chest and felt his tongue in her mouth. Had heard his heart beating faster as she explored his body. She recalled her own reactions to his touch. She had never been aroused so fast in her life. Had never felt the painful need to be touched like that. The feeling struck deeper than carnal lust, though. A familiarity lurked there: like it wouldn't be a sin to want him like that because she had him before.

She inhaled and exhaled as the instructor told her and tried to calm herself. This was not the place to lose herself over a dark, mysterious, handsome smile. The instructor stood up, putting her foot on the inside of her thigh, and lifted her arms. When she inhaled, Brigit following her movements, something happened.

She thought at first that the sun just peeked through the Ohio clouds and illuminated the teacher. Her shadow on the wall behind her signaled otherwise. The instructor smiled and suddenly the whole room felt relaxed and peaceful. She felt a warmth seep into her as she inhaled and slowed her heart down. Relax, the atmosphere said, and she did.

Around the instructor, a kind of fuzzy, golden glow illuminated the space around her. It pulsed very faintly, but Brigit could make it out, like dust in the sun just around her, and it gave the illusion of pulsing outwards. Like what some described an aura to look like. When she finished holding the pose, it faded, and Brigit felt her muscles tense up again.

"Did you see that?" she whispered to Mary.

"How relaxed you got? Yeah, it was great." She smiled.

"No, I felt that too. I mean the teacher. She was practically glowing."

"Aw," Mary cooed. "That's what this can do for you. I knew this was a good idea. Way to go, Brigit. Soon, you'll be glowing too!"

"No!" She hissed now. "She was literally glowing."

Fortunately, the class ended then. Brigit continued to hiss in Mary's ear as they left the studio.

"Maybe I'm going crazy," she suggested simply. "People don't glow."

"They do when they're happy," Mary suggested.

"Not that kind of glow!" She picked up the pace. "Forget it. I'm going to the library, okay? See you later."

"What about the shop?" Mary called.

"It can wait a day. It's Sunday; who cares?"

S he practically sprinted to the library around the corner and went into the mythology section. She knew it well because back when they were in college, they spent most of their time there pouring over books about fairies, goblins, and wizards. Today, she had to return to that section and submerge herself back into that part of her life that she recently turned her nose up at. Magic was for people who couldn't handle real life.

She opened up an older book with golden pages and orange symbols on the cover. This had been her favorite as a college kid. It burst with illustrations, stories and how-tos for finding fairies in the backyard. She flipped to the section she was looking for. There it was: Glow. She read:

"Some fairies came across to the human world for purposes of their own, but they could be spotted when in great emotion by the glowing aura around them. This aura can have many effects on mortal humans. Some may feel elated, some may fall in love, some may feel at ease or as if the world is theirs. This is specific to neutral or good spirits and is experienced in different ways by dark spirits. To see the aura of a fairy is not unlike reading the aura of a human..."

She glossed over where it went on to talk about how the fairies on this side of the veil needed to consume something called glow to stay in touch with such powers. On the next page, a drawing of a triskelion that Ildanach wore on his belt lay hidden among other runes and symbols. She knew it was a common design. This time the sight of it made her heat tingle now. She had almost had that off of him just the night before. He had touched her but denied her the same pleasure.

Realizing this, she snapped the book shut and made up her mind that next time, it wouldn't be a one-sided deal. No, she wanted to touch him, too. Arouse him the way he had her. She wanted him under her, panting and craving her touch. She stopped and realized she started breathing too loud and an old woman across the way stared at her with a very judgmental look on her face for interrupting the silence. She pushed her hair back and walked out, not ashamed, and ignored the stare that followed her.

When she got back to her shop, she opened the catalogue she usually ordered from and ordered several titles for her bookshelf. She realized she didn't have a lot of books on the Celtic lore of magic and decided that would be a good addition to her store. She could show them to Ildanach. She wondered if he ever flipped through books. Imagining him as a bookish kind of guy made her secretly smile.

She looked down at his business card near her register. The address was on the bottom left-hand corner. She could call and see if her car was ready. Or she could show up at his yard and see the business that somehow managed to get him a great truck and terrific sound system. It wasn't too far out of town. She'd probably have to take a cab, though. And then he'd have to drive her home. To her place. Alone.

She quickly snapped up her bag and jacket, dialing the nearest cab company with quivering fingers.

Chapter 13

The Hunters

Just after dropping Brigit off that night, Ildanach had to pose as a substitute night watchman at the elementary school in order to legally gain access to the supposedly haunted halls. He had nearly forgotten about his planned investigation after the time with Brigit. Even though it hadn't gone the way he wanted it to. That was his fault, right? He could have let it go and enjoyed himself. Brigit made it clear that she would have let him, too. Her encouragement was a good sign. That came second next to the fact that she had the glow inside her. Even that felt like it could be put aside compared to how he felt about her. Her anger at the world and confusion somehow attracted him. Perhaps because she didn't let it consume her. She didn't need him. She thrived along, so self-sufficient and strong. She'd gotten this far in her life alone, and it hadn't been easy. She had the strength.

A noise down the hall alerted him to his mission. Mischievous and small-time rogue spirits often masqueraded as ghosts or demons to humans. He came to the school to take one down that took on the guise of a girl who supposedly drowned in a well years before the school existed. The story, while true, attracted fairies who wanted to frighten mortals. Some spirits were far more dangerous and would harm a human if given the chance. Like Arawn. He'd save that boy from before. Still, he couldn't help wondering what would have happened if he was too late. Or if Arawn went after more people than he could save. He prayed things weren't heating up that dangerously.

Ildanach took out his iron dagger from under his false security guise and pressed himself into the wall. The spirit knew another presence approached without seeing him, though it would never know he too was a fairy. It would disguise itself as the ghost of a drowned girl, thinking a mortal had wandered in. He hoped it was just a rogue spirit and not one of the angry ones. He didn't want to kill it. Threatening it with iron would hopefully make it leave the school alone. At least for a little while. Otherwise, he could use a banishing spell to force it back behind the veil. Those were last resort though. Never pleasant.

He peeked around the corner and saw it. A white outline of a mortal, wearing modern clothes and wandering down the hall as though lost. It sniffed and cried, making an eerie sound as it shuffled along. The sobs echoed and lilted in pitch down the hallway. Taking a breath, he stepped out and brandished the knife.

"Lost your way, fairy?" he smirked.

The spirit shivered and wavered before his face. He frowned. It was a little ghost boy, not a dripping girl from the late 1800s.

"Changed your disguise, I see." It was more of a question, but he wanted to keep his tone strong.

"I'm lost," the ghost boy said. "I thought I knew where I was going. I can't seem to find my way."

He looked too normal. A modern-day band t-shirt, Converses on his feet, and a "I love zombies" bracelet on. A very modern boy.

"Nice try, pixie. Stop messing around, I've a schedule to keep. Get out of here before sunup or I'll make you."

The ghost boy burst into raw, unearthly tears, his sobs eerie and distorted. "There was a dog, and I ran away from it. The man said I'd see my dad again. It bit me." He held up his wrists and Ildanach froze. On the boy's wrists were the bite marks of a hound.

"What happened?" he asked cautiously, lowering the iron blade.

"I was being chased, then I fell. The dog got me, and the man said it would be okay. Said if I let go, I'll see my dad again. I can't find him!" He wiped his eyes with his hand. "I ran here because it's the best place I know to hide. He scared me."

"You like school?" Ildanach asked gently. "So, you came here." He frowned in thought. A stone settled in his stomach as he realized what happened.

Arawn really had been ripping souls out of mortal's bodies. Not taking them. Ildanach thought perhaps he was just bored and started collecting them for a diversion, enjoying his oppression tactics. If he abandoned souls, letting them wander on the mortal's side of the veil, something else was afoot. It didn't make sense, but there it was. Plain as reality. This boy could be just one of many wandering souls, left to frighten the living, forever lost in an eternal hell. The ethereal did not mix well with the mortal. If human spirits were allowed to roam free, there was no limit to the horrific things that could take place. Real hauntings. Scared ghosts, provoked into killing. The humans would go mad with fright.

"Listen," he bent down to be on the child's level. "I have a friend who might be able to help you. I need you to wait here. In a closet or something. Don't talk to anyone. Especially that old man again. Wait for my friend. He'll tell you his name is Robin. He's a messenger for me and for someone far more powerful than me. Can you do that?"

The boy sniffed and nodded.

Ildanach left instantly. He had to attend a debriefing of other fairies after banishing the rogue spirit, and he had to tell them about this.

He went straight to the meeting point - a hotel room in town - and waited for the others. He changed while he waited, not wanting them to know the levels to which he had to stoop in order to protect the mortals. They were high fairies, after all. The suite expanded over the top of the hotel: two bedrooms, a living room, and a small kitchen off to the side. It was the best hotel in town, but he expected the high fairies to make comments about how dismal it was compared to others.

"Ildanach," a voice purred behind him as he watched the humans out the window of the hotel. He turned to see Aine, the guardian of agriculture who used to reign supreme in the Celtic world. She had white hair and the slightest of wrinkles in the corners of her blue eyes. She swayed in with the gentle movements of a stalk of wheat blowing in the wind. "I love seeing how the mortal world has not affected you in the least. Your glow is strong. That is good."

"How are you these days?" he asked lightly. "Still living in Ireland?"

Aine breathed in heavily and sighed. "The magic is stronger there." She winced, looking out the window as the sanitation crew cascaded the trash from the dumpster into their compactor. "How can you stand it here?"

A strong knock came through the living room door. Before either answered, the doors thrust open, and two more men came in. The one who had not waited to be invited in led the way. He stood taller than the others and had long brown hair that hung to his waist. His eyes were nearly neon green with glow and power. His skin was brown and smooth.

"Herne, why do you never wait to be invited in?" Ildanach asked. "Aine and I could have been making out." He winked at her, and she turned her nose up at him, chiding him like a child.

"The great god can do as he wishes," said the singsong voice of the other man. Oison, the fairy of songs and stories, never intimidated Ildanach and he could never remember seeing him in a bad mood. He had fiery red hair and lavender eyes. "Ildanach, how can you live here? I hear the humans' minds all day and am bored with their trifling thoughts. Not one of them dreams up something he cannot see for fear of ridicule."

"Your standards are high, Oison," Ildanach smiled. "I do have urgent business to discuss."

"Guardians," Aine sniffed. "Always in a hurry. You are too mortal, Ildanach."

"Have I displeased the fairy court?" Ildanach asked. He held no real concern, but had to play the politics and keep the big people happy.

"Nothing of the sort," Herne said in his deep, earthy voice. He slowly measured Ildanach with his searching eyes. The high ones were slow. They had millennia of time to spare.

Nothing could be hidden from Herne. Nothing. Ildanach could feel him reading his thoughts even now. He had drunk extra glow to try to protect his mind from the greater fairies. It still proved useless against Herne. He knew everything now. The ghost boy, Arawn, what Robin had wanted for breakfast, and...Brigit.

Herne's eye turned from scrutiny and elation to sadness. "Our guardian wants to leave us," he said suddenly, interrupting something Aine had been saying. Ildanach stood respectfully by while the great spirit spoke. "You know our laws, Ildanach," he went on. "A guardian may give up his immortality. Why would you want to?" He seemed genuinely saddened by what he read in Ildanach's mind. He didn't understand.

Ildanach licked his lips. He couldn't expect them to understand. There was no way. They were too powerful. Too old.

"I have lived many lifetimes," he began, looking each in the eye as he spoke. "Each time I live, I love, I fight, I lose. I am always the same. My quest becomes to find my love. You know this. It has always been this way. She is born, grows, we find each other. Every time, her mortal flesh passes. I remain."

Aine rolled her blue eyes. "We know. You have only moaned about it more and more each hundred years or so."

"I am finished," Ildanach said flatly. "I have found her, and I can end it. I... want to stop. To pass the torch."

Oison's eyes filled with sadness as well. "It's a lovely story,

Ildanach. If you leave, another guardian must take your place if you chose..." he swallowed. "If you choose a mortal life to be with her. One last time."

"There is no afterlife for you," Herne said sadly. "You will die." His eyes clouded and grew very serious. "And so will she. Are you ready to take that from her? If she knows who you are, who she is, and chooses death with you, she will die."

"Who?" Aine burst suddenly. "Ildanach, my boy, have you found the exalted one? Have you found Brighid? Your Brighid?"

Ildanach nodded. He couldn't tell them the rest. Couldn't even admit to himself what his choice honestly meant. "And I love her. More than I ever have before."

"She will none," Herne said suddenly. Ildanach hated how much he could read minds. "She is not a believer in anything beyond what she can see. She will not have it, Ildanach. You may die for nothing."

Aine put her hand over her heart. "Don't do it, young guardian. Live more, again, and find her anew. She will return."

Ildanach's heart began to break. His own people wouldn't heed him. Wouldn't support him. Was he wrong? Making a stupid decision and being selfish? Maybe he should stay and protect the earth for another thousand years or so. His heart tore between her and this world, and his world of immortality.

Herne saw Ildanach's face twist as he fought to argue. "It cannot be done, young guardian."

"What do you care? I'm replaceable!" Ildanach said more forcefully than he meant to. He didn't regret saying it: guardians came and went. But these fairies—they were thousands, if not billions of years old. They saw the situation far differently than he did.

The horned god sighed deeply. "Arawn travels his own path - a path beyond our borders. Giving up your life, and Brighid's life, is not worth it. You must prove your love and sacrifice yourself upon a sacred altar to lock Arawn away." He held out his hands slowly. "I see your life is worth more than all mortals he has tortured and killed."

That decided it to them. The other great ones didn't move or show any motion that they would continue to discuss Ildanach sacrificing himself and Brigit.

"If we cannot speak on that matter, may I speak of the glow?" he asked instead. "Robin has reported that – "

"Bastard fairy!" Aine cut in.

Herne quieted her with a glare. Ildanach went on.

"Robin has reported that the ones who travel between our world and this are no longer able to bring it. You know what that substance means to us on this side of the veil." He looked at Herne now. "Why are they not bringing it?"

"Glow is precious," Herne said. It sounded like the opening to a speech. "You think you need it in this world."

"We do!" Ildanach said quickly. He had probably spent too much time on this side of the veil, thinking sometimes Herne acted like a thick-headed CEO of a corporation; he had no idea what went on in the workplace and gave out orders without thinking of the workers.

"The humans are less worthy of your power, guardian. You may find that you can do your job without it. And," he said louder when Ildanach tried to interrupt, "you grow dependent on it. Yes, you desire it too much. I think, Ildanach, you will find the strength you already possess is more than enough."

"What?" Ildanach said. "I don't have the patience for your cryptic words these days, Herne."

The great spirit nodded, his semi-visible crown of antlers brushing the hanging chandelier above them. "I see that. I think I will leave this for you to decipher. You have the power, guardian, to do all you need. Do not be dependent."

He turned and Ildanach couldn't believe he was leaving. Herne motioned the other two to follow him out.

"Is that it?" Ildanach called after them. But they were gone, vanished back to the other side of the veil.

He took his hat off and ran his hand through his long hair. Meetings like that infuriated him. Why were elder spirits always so damn cryptic and closed-mouthed?

He had to get back to his place. Tired from the long day before, he didn't want to think any more. He drove slowly through town on his bike, trying not to fall asleep while his brain reeled in mysteries. Herne had said he had all the power he needed. Without the glow, he wouldn't die, but no healing, no mental protection from other fairies, and worst of all, his aura would fade. He'd lose his inner light. Like that fairy in the Peter Pan book. He'd fade out.

On top of these worries sat Arawn. Had that dark rogue spirit crossed the line into being his problem? *Of course, he is, you're the guardian after all,* he told himself. So he had to choose. Fight Arawn for eternity or love Brigit. His Brigit, as Aine had put it. Give up his light, immortality, for her. Would she ever gain her memories back and know him? Would she want to live just once more with him? It was the only way to imprison the rogue spirit once again. Other fae had given their lives to hold off much smaller threats.

These questions were still spinning in his mind when he got back to his yard and stumbled in the door, disoriented with fatigue.

"Ildanach, someone called," Robin said, running after his master with a note pad. "Are you okay?"

"A rum and coke, Robin," he muttered, flopping onto his bed, not bothering to change. "And make me some instant ramen."

Robin squinted in disgust. "Ok, Nach. You were out all night and this morning, though." He went over and pulled his thick, black leather boots off and rolled him over onto the bed properly.

"There was a ghost," Ildanach sighed. "Trapped."

Robin looked up through his red brows. "A real one? That's...not right."

"It's not. I can't do anything about it. Not yet. He's just trapped there, Robin. Waiting."

Sensing they were about to enter dangerous, emotional territory, Robin skipped to the back kitchen area to avoid any exhaustion-driven conversation he knew his master would regret later. He wanted to tell him Brigit called, however the side of him that was still Puck the pixie wanted her to come over and see the great man eating ramen and drinking rum at ten in the morning. With a mischievous smile, he closed the door and went to fetch the disgusting breakfast.

Chapter 14

Junk Yard

The wind picked up like it always did this time of year in Ohio. It blew bitter, harsh, and cold. Brigit wrapped a scarf around her chin, but her face and eyes still burned as she waited for the taxi. She and her father had hated winter. Not her mother. "It is the time of the frost fairies!" she would say. "The Green Man sleeps and out comes Jack Frost."

She had never understood about death, even when it came to trees and winter. "Why does Jack kill everything?" she had asked every winter as a child. One particularly long winter, she also lost her puppy to a sledding accident and decided that winter was the worst. To help console her, her mother had introduced the Yule log.

"Keep this burning until Christmas," she had said when they lit it in the grate. Her father had protested. Neither of them paid him any mind. "Whenever you look at it, remember that our world and the next are connected. There is a little glowing ember in this life, too, Brig. You just have to find them before they return to the fairyland."

Brigit smiled as she rode in the taxi. Remembering her

mother started to get easier. She hadn't seen her much in the last few years. Still, her death rattled her mentally and shaken the grounds on which she had tried to create a belief system. Maybe this year, she'd get a Yule log again. If only the people she rented from would let her burn something that big. Maybe she could claim religious reasons?

No, that was ridiculous. She'd pass it up just like she had for many years now. Fairyland existed for that poor Brigit who missed her dog. What if Henry died? Maybe then she'd light a candle in mourning. She didn't really know.

The thought of glowing embers reminded her of what she had seen that morning in the yoga class. She wanted to deny it with all of her heart, but her eyes hadn't lied. There was no way. She was so sure of what she had seen. Maybe she was just too wrapped up in this new desire for hope and a new life.

Burying her past gave her one chance. And then Ildanach had walked into her life. A real relationship always meant big change; one she had wanted for years. Mary believed whole-heartedly in love and romance. Why couldn't Brigit?

Because I want reality, she thought. She couldn't even tell what that was, though.

"Okay, cut it out," she mumbled to herself. "You are getting way out of hand with these ideas." Ildanach was real. She had felt him in her arms. Maybe that was a safer place to dream.

The cabbie let her out in front of a large gate. The fence went all the way around what appeared to be a graveyard filled with everything from elephant-sized machines to dead motorcy-cles the size of deer. There were a few little garages scattered throughout and one large, three-story building in the very center. The iron on the gate and the fence were rusted to the point of being brittle.

Brigit's heart fell a little. She double-checked the business card. Nope, this was the right address. But how? Everything else he owned, the way he dressed—everything said, "I make money." It didn't really change how she felt about him. A lot could be said about a man who, literally, lived in a junkyard. There didn't seem to be anything magical about his home. She had rather hoped there would be. In fact, it resembled a kind of fortress, like he tried to keep something out.

Taking a brave breath, she pushed the gate, and it swung open. She made sure to close it in case he had any dogs. At this point, that wouldn't surprise her. Despite the decay and junk around her, a walkway curved throughout the clutter, paved with smooth, grey stones.

A glowing open sign on the front door of the middle building showed her where to go. She wondered how customers were supposed to know how to get there or that the place wasn't abandoned. The door wasn't dirty, so she wasted no time in pushing it open and entering. The inside shined clean too, to her surprise. A desk with no one in it greeted her. The strangest thing was the feeling of the building. Stepping over the threshold, she suddenly felt like a burden been lifted off her chest and grew lightheaded. She stifled a girlish giggle.

When she looked harder, she noticed crystals hanging innocently in the windows. There were also little bunches of lavender and tiny runes hanging by the doors. At the base of the structure, where the walls met the floor, a line created a barrier of white grains that looked like salt. She crouched down to get a better look, her mind reeling with curiosity.

"Goblins cannot cross salt lines," a high voice said from behind the desk.

"Ah!" She shot up and turned around, totally unaware of the short young man behind the desk. He had an impish look about himself. He looked goblin-like and cute at the same time. Long, tasseled red hair, a thin nose, and slightly triangular ears.

"I'm sorry, I didn't see you," she said. He'd been sitting there, and she just missed him?

"So long as you weren't stealing anything, who cares?" He shrugged and smiled brightly, almost knowingly.

She slowly bit her lower lip, not sure how to reply. A very strange and awkward silence followed. The redhead just stared at her, a smile pulling his thin lips that would have worked much better on a psychopath's face.

"Uh, goblins?" she asked, pointing to the salt.

The redhead shrugged again. "Or maybe it's just cockroach poison." He winked at her as though expecting her to get some joke he alluded to. When she said nothing, his smile faded a little.

"Oh, that makes sense," she offered nervously.

"What can I help you with today?" he asked.

Well, at least there are people working here, she thought. "I was looking for the guy that owns this place. His name is on this card, and he has my car. Fixing the front bumper, a light, fender, and the hood I think."

The little imp-like boy's face suddenly brightened.

"Ooooh," he said slowly. "You're Brigit Elderbrook." He nodded. "Now I see why you don't know about salt. Or do you?" He squinted at her.

"What?" she asked, growing agitated.

"Tell me, Brigit," he came out from behind the counter and leaned on the desk, facing her. "Do I look like the great god Pan? You know, the faun?"

"Uh, no. More like Peter Pan. He was pretty cool, too," she added on after a second.

"I just think I have some god-like qualities; you know what I mean?" He raised a well-manicured eyebrow at her and winked again.

The level of discomfort rose to record heights as she winced. "Um, sure, I mean, I don't know."

"Robin, shut the hell up!" a familiar voice shouted from the back. Even his annoyed grumbling sounded sexy.

The young man, Robin, squeaked, giggled, and ran back behind the desk where he suddenly put on a show of looking busy. Some crashing sounds and heavy footsteps from down the hall preceded a wonderful sight.

Brigit gaped silently when she saw Ildanach. He stumbled in from apparently sleeping on a couch, rubbing his neck and stretching. His belt hung loose around his waist, no longer clasped. The top button of his black jeans undone. He was gloriously shirtless, showing a smooth and muscled chest, almost glowing in the afternoon sun. His shoulders were knotted with just enough muscle to make her want to kiss them. His hair, brushing them gently, shined its dark color in the light.

He froze when he saw her. Not prepared to see her in his own home, his face paled, turning vulnerable as she stared and judged him. She knew he felt uneasy, but she couldn't take her eyes away. She stared hard. Mary would be so jealous.

"I came to check on my car," she said weakly. She could hardly hear her own words. Her knees were going to give out.

Her heart might stop beating. *Stop looking,* she chided herself. She wanted to touch his stomach. Brush her fingers over his arms and give him goosebumps. She wanted to make him moan. She wanted to hear him panting in her ear, call her name, gasp when she made him climax.

She dropped her eyes to the floor.

"I'll show you," he said casually. He reached to the chair beside the wall where a pile of laundry waited - no doubt a task of Robin's gone forgotten - and pulled out a shirt. To her dismay, he slipped it on and then led her out into the yard behind the building.

She wanted to speak. Something to fill the silence between their crunching footsteps. After her thoughts just then, though, she didn't trust her voice. Still, she had to know his thoughts. He had touched her, made her gasp, and now he seemed to have forgotten about it. What had the night before been to him?

"Sorry about my entrance back there," he said suddenly. He smiled and ran his fingers through his glossy locks. "I had a really, really late night and an early morning and had passed out on the couch. Guess I was more stressed than I thought." His voice sounded light. She could see the truth in his eyes. He did look tired.

"Junk business got you stressed out?" she smiled back.

"Hey." He stopped and took her hand. She tensed, the smile sliding from her face quickly. "That may be the first real smile I've seen on your face." He looked into her eyes like he always did: deeply, without letting out his thoughts, reading hers.

He smiled through one side of his perfect lips and held her hand as he led her into the garage where her car waited. A box sat on the hood and a larger one on the ground. Neither had been opened yet.

"I was hoping you'd not lost interest after last night," he said.

Glad he brought it up, a little tension eased. "I think I understood," she offered. "Really, you can't blame a girl for wondering."

"What is it?" he asked.

"I know you said I didn't do anything wrong, but you left me in kind of a lurch. What am I supposed to think?"

"That there's a reason I haven't opened these parts yet." He tapped one of the boxes with his hand. "I got the parts almost right away for your car."

And here they had sat, she realized. He could have had the car out the next day. He had chosen not to.

"I wanted to see you," he said, softly moving closer to her.

He pressed his legs against hers and kissed the top of her head. She felt him breathe her in while he nuzzled her hair. He put one hand on her back and the other, caressed on the side of her face.

"Forgive me?" he whispered. "I know you must be angry. Can you trust me?"

"Trust you?" she said in a husky voice. He was affecting her. Her mouth had gone dry. "Why do we have to wait?"

"This is a strange turn of events." He smiled. He kissed her forehead and then the bridge of her nose. His hands cupped her shoulders. "Isn't this conversation usually the other way around?"

She put her hand on his chest, a little saddened by the plea to wait again. "I suppose. Why can't you tell me what's wrong?"

"There's nothing wrong," he insisted. "I just have to finalize a few things before..."

Brigit rolled her eyes but giggled, realizing what his hesitation must be. "Well, I'm glad to hear that."

"What?"

"You have commitment issues just like every other guy. You're just a regular." She laid her head on his chest.

"Don't you want commitment?" he asked.

She didn't reply. Of course. Who didn't? But a fling couldn't hurt.

Damn! She chided herself. She couldn't fool herself. He had the disposition she didn't; had every quality she lacked. She wanted him. Every part of him. And she wanted him for keeps. Couldn't lie to herself anymore. Her father had been a non-commitment type man, and that was the last kind of man she wanted in her life. She wanted a forever. She needed a forever.

"Yeah, I do." Her voice cracked, the emotion showing through. "I'm sorry." A single tear trickled down her cheek. She tried to pull away, but his arms were there, binding her to him, not going to let her go. Not now, not later. Not ever. She could hear it in his heartbeat.

"I guess I don't know what I want." She sniffed.

They sunk down together, leaning against her car; she nestled in his arms as he simply listened. She hadn't felt this safe in a long time. This comforted.

"I want to be happy. I feel like I can't allow myself to be. Not with my family and the accident. Not my father and him ignoring us. How can I be happy when all that is going on?"

"Why not?" Ildanach asked tenderly. He tucked her hair

behind one ear and laid his cheek against her head. "Don't think for one second you don't deserve it."

"I think I don't!" The tears flowed now, and she couldn't stop them. This right now was not what she had in mind when she decided to sneak up on the man she might be falling in love with. "Does that make me bad?" She hiccupped and blushed at the embarrassing noise. "I feel like there's more to me than this." She motioned to her body. "Like I've forgotten something, and the thing that I've forgotten is the reason I have to be happy. Like nothing that makes me sad matters anyway. I can't find it."

Ildanach turned her face to him and wiped her tears. She closed her eyes and relished the feel of him wiping away her sadness. His hands were warm.

"No, it doesn't make you bad." He pulled her close and held her.

They sat like this for some time, Brigit calming down and loving his exotic smell. Maybe she wanted this all along. It felt right. She fit into his arms and against his chest too perfectly. She felt as though all the other guys she'd ever dated were just wrong and incomplete compared to this one moment. Being in his arms, listening to his heart match hers beat for beat, she felt whole. They didn't have to undress, make each other moan - this felt better. Pure comfort and protection.

"Brigit, let me promise you something." Ildanach's voice had changed. She heard his heart pick up pace as he spoke. His muscles tensed. His breaths shortened and came faster. "I swear, no matter what happens, to be with you through this lifetime."

She sat up, confusion on her face as she stared into his eyes. His eyes were strangely intense. So intense, she thought she could see fear, passion, fire, and wonder behind his gaze all at once. The fear? What was that about?

"I will be yours if you will be mine, no matter the storms. No power can pull apart what we've chosen shall be together. I swear. No matter..." he swallowed hard. His face darkened, turning so brave. "No matter what happens."

A smile of relief and joy broke her face and made her eyes shut in happiness. On the surface, that turn came quickly. Underneath, she knew she had waited a lifetime to hear those words. An ache inside her that festered for years washed away. She couldn't explain it. That didn't matter. She threw her arms around his neck and hugged him close.

"For that," she purred, "I'd wait a lifetime if you want."

Chapter 15

A Rip In The Veil

The dancing figures in Stonehenge flared before her again. She hadn't dreamt it in days now, and she did not miss it. It used to be just eerie: dark outlines of writhing, dancing people around the stones. Now she felt things. A fire blazed somewhere in a towering, triangle shape. Away from it, the cold night air kissed her skin. She would usually try to shrink away from the dream when it got more vivid. This time she couldn't. She began to panic as she realized she dreamt, paralyzed. Her body screamed, "No, let me stay!" As the words ripped from her throat, she realized her body didn't say it: *she* did.

She moved into the midst of the fire and dancers, panting, sweating. Her thighs and stomach churning as though she just come away from the most passionate, forbidden sex she had ever had. She wasn't enjoying the sex anymore; two men in primitive armor with long swords at their sides pulled her away and into the audience.

"I've found him. Please, don't take me! I must stay!" she shrieked. Her voice, wracked with sobs, carried over the crowd as she begged to remain with him. Dragged before a host of royally clad people who stood on a pedestal, she looked up through her messy hair. If their robes had not been decaying and handing in ghostly wisps, she would have thought them Old English nobility.

"You, woman, we have found you out," an older man with long white hair shouted down to her. At his side sat a great hound with fire hovering just over its burning flesh, with glowing coals for eyes. "I know what magic you weave here, and I will have none of it!"

"You bastard!" she spat and saw blood mingled with her spittle. "What I do here tonight is for all mankind." Her body ached; bruised, bloodied, and beaten. "I lay with a man I love to keep you from this earth! With our vows and our act of love, we bind you!" she screeched, far more courageous than she felt. "You come to corrupt, to persecute, and drive a wedge not only between the new Christians and our old ways, but between these mortals who cannot see us and our world."

"You are a goddess to these people!" the old man shouted back, his voice tearing his throat in anger. "Why would you take their shape? Bow to their ideals, take on their animalistic ways and lie with a lesser being—a guardian?"

Brigit laughed bitterly as a smirk curved up a corner of her lips. Naivety didn't spark his question, anger did. "You know my magic, dark walker. I bring life. The guardian I lie with brings protection. Us two joined will bar you from this side of the veil for our lifetime. Better that than to love on our side, in our world, and let you wander free here."

A dull ache crept through her legs as she knelt before this pitiful host of underworld fairies. If the mortals in celebration around them witnessed their goddess this way, they may have lost faith. That is what she fought for. What she sacrificed for.

"Many lifetimes have I evaded you," said the man, his voice low, still audible over the chaos around them. "How many times, Brigit, oh goddess of life, have you been reborn into a human body to find your love on this side of the veil? Take him back with you now, appoint another guardian, and live together forever. Your battle is over."

Again, Brigit spat into the green grass. "I must have the faith these mortals lack and keep you out," she answered, putting as much venom into her words as she could. "The guardian will never let you have this earth!"

At this, the man laughed. Softly at first, then it grew until he neared hysteria.

"What mirth do you find?" she demanded. Fear gripped her ribs and crunched them together. Had something happened to her love? There couldn't be. He was a fairy, the same as her; immortal. What happened?

"I have pushed him into the sight of mortals," the old man said at last.

"No!" Brigit fought against the two guards holding her down.

"Now that he has been there, he must stay. As is our law. He will be the guardian. For eternity. No longer will he be able to protect them from this side. He must harvest glow for himself if he wishes to remain strong. You have made his task so much harder than it needed to be, dear goddess."

He raised his eyebrows and widened his eyes with a

hunter's gleam. "I can kill him now. Iron in his heart, perhaps? A hound to chew on his bones... The options are endless and my reign over earth has just begun. So early too. The mortal's calendars haven't even started yet."

"No!" Brigit cried as the black host vanished into the fire. "No, he cannot be exiled. I will find him! I will be born again! Wait for me, Ildanach!"

B rigit's phone vibrated its way off the nightstand by the time the alarm trilled loudly next to it. She kicked off her many blankets and rubbed her eyes. That dream had been the worst of the bunch. Many dreams involving magic, fire, and stone circles, and any number of other weird things had occurred in the past, but that was certainly the worst. In this one, she called for Ildanach by name. Licking her lips, she realized it hadn't been limited to the dream. Her throat burned dry, and her body exhausted. She easily believed that she had lived through the whole dream.

She had had some awesome sex in that dream. Rubbing her fingers together, she could recall his touch as though she'd felt it a million times before. She knew him, his body, and what he liked. Her dream man liked to be kissed on the neck during foreplay. And he didn't mind her nails on his back when she came. He had long, dark hair that she often ran her fingers through...

"Enough is enough!" she said aloud. Across the room, Henry begged her to keep her voice down and reminded her that ferrets need at least fifteen hours of sleep. "I'm sorry, baby," she sighed, rubbing her eyes again. The figures weren't leaving her vision.

Remembering her phone, she quickly snapped it up and read the line of texts. Her heart jumped when she saw Ildanach's name on her screen. Before she left, she had snapped his picture to show up when he called or texted. The candid image made him look adorable. He smiled into it, bleary-eyed and frizzly haired, from whatever his rough night the day before brought. Seeing that side of him made him a little more accessible and within her reach. His smile was still mysterious and soft.

"Car's old, I may have chipped the paint," the text read.

She giggled, and her toes curled up in utter giddiness. Sighing happily, she fell back into her cool pillows and read the next one.

"And I thought I overslept!" with a little laughing face after it.

How could he be so dark and quiet, yet so light and wonderful? She scrolled through the next three. He gave her an update about her car, said he dropped her hood on his foot, and that Robin wanted her to bring donuts if she came to visit. She sighed deeply again. Her face hurt from grinning. She didn't mind at all. Her heart felt whole and healed. He had promised himself to her. Sure, there was still a lot of time to get to know each other, but she had never felt so involved with a man before. Never felt the urgency.

Deciding she could daydream while on the job, she ate a quick breakfast, fed Henry, and took him down to the shop below. She skipped down the stairs, singing *Stop in the Name of Love* and swinging Henry's little cage around to the beat. She reached the chorus when she came to the back wall to flip on the lights.

Her phone rang, and she squealed when she saw Ildanach's name.

"Excuse me, Henry, I know you want all of my attention and love, but I must take this. I have so many suitors, you see." She blew him a kiss and answered her phone. "Hi," she said, trying to contain her joy.

Across the street Mary waved to her, stalling when she saw her preoccupied with the phone, then mimicked screaming joy when Brigit mouthed Ildanach's name. Mary applauded her silently.

"I thought you wouldn't answer," he said over the phone. "I was texting you all morning. You said don't call often, so I wasn't, but then you don't answer."

She smiled and couldn't keep it out of her voice. "I was having crazy dreams last night. You wouldn't believe them. Well, maybe *you* would. You like that kind of thing."

"Oh, really?" His tone became genuinely curious. "What were you dreaming of? Good or bad?"

"Funny you should ask. It was good at first. I think anyway. Then it got bad..." she stalled out.

She went back to the storage room to finish turning on the light and unlock the door when something caught her eye. Shiny, shattered pieces of mirror sprinkled the ground. Gasping, she looked up and saw the magic mirror, smashed. Thinking something must have fallen on it, she checked the shelves. Everything still hung or rested where it should be.

She glanced around, realizing someone must have broken in again. Like before, nothing was stolen. She took a step back and stumbled over a large metal object on the floor. Shaking some of the glass off her foot, she bent and scooped it up: a large, iron stiletto with a ribbon tied on it that didn't belong to her. Her hand shaking, she held it up to read some handwritten message on the ribbon. It said, "No belief is disbelief. Death is imminent."

"What the hell?" she breathed. All around her feet, paw prints tracked over the wooden floor, burned into it.

Chapter 16

Tilt

"Brigit?" Ildanach shouted into the phone for the tenth time. She didn't answer. He could hear her walking and mumbling, but there no words filtered through he could make out. "What is it?"

She hung up. He knew she'd never hang up on him like that without it being important. She could either be in danger or frightened, and he would tolerate neither of those.

"Robin, lock everything up, fortify the fence again, and make sure all the talismans are hanging up properly," he barked out as he gathered his utility belt, hat, and coat.

"Walking near iron makes me ill," Robin complained. "I'm not as strong as you."

"Do it," Ildanach ordered. "I don't know what's going on. Can't you feel it now?"

"I feel your anxiety," Robin said, handing him his sling and hat. "You need to calm down. This is Jennifer all over again."

"Jennifer wasn't it. I just thought she was. In the years since her, I've come to realize I forced it. Not this time."

"Yeah, you never talked about her incessantly like you do this girl. Gloves," he handed them to Ildanach when he saw his master looking frantically for them before picking up the iron blade.

"She is Brigit. She has the name. And this time...I recognize her. Whether or not she regains her past's memories, I still love her. And I can never love like this again, Robin. Not for another lifetime."

Robin's round, green eyes filled with fear, and his jaw dropped. "Ildanach, no!" he gasped. "You can't give up your immortality for her. Not while she's just a mortal. The spell doesn't work like that; she has to know who she is! You'll die and Arawn will still be free!" He clutched the front of Ildanach's coat, begging him to reconsider. "I mean, that's why you've not done the deed, right? Because of the spell?"

Ildanach pried the frightened pixie's fingers loose. "There is an afterlife. If we die together as old mortals, so be it. I know we cannot cage Arawn and his hounds if she has not regained her power. That's not what I want. I want to love her even if we cannot defeat him."

"That's so selfish!" Robin shook his head. "Your job is to protect us all. If you give up your mortality, no amount of glow in the earth, what's left, can help you. You'll be with the woman you love, but she won't know you. Our world will be vulnerable while Arawn's still out there!" Fear shone in his eyes. Ildanach had no idea what he might be doing. "She'll be dead before you anyhow!"

Ildanach didn't have time for Robin's worries, but he couldn't leave him like this. Not after the centuries of servitude he had suffered with him. He focused on the pixie's face and said gently, "Robin, I swear I will not leave you and our kind unprotected."

He reached down to the pixie's neck and removed the necklace that matched his own. "I hold your debt fulfilled, Robin Goodfellow. Tell the Oberon and Herne I have released you and you may claim sanctuary in my estate on the other side of the veil. It is for you to do with as you will. I won't be needing it. You're free." He tossed the amulet aside and took his hat, preparing to leave.

"I can't leave yet," Robin sighed. "I have to fortify the fences and make sure this place is safe. Bring her here. It's far more protected than you can make her hovel in time."

Ildanach smiled, relieved to have Robin's loyalty still. He was right. This place would be safer for Brigit to hide while he investigated what threatened her.

"Thank you, my friend."

He pulled the cord from under his hat where it normally resided and tightened it on his chin to keep it from flying off as he sped on his bike through the small wilderness of the Ohio fields and woods. His heart raced and his mind reeled with the worst possibilities. It could have just been a mortal attacking her store. Wouldn't she have noticed sooner? The front door would have been broken or the other window smashed.

He should really replace that for her. He should tell her how he broke it.

***

His senses were on high alert when he entered town. The sun had come out today, the wind was harsh as always, however no sense of threat flowed to him on the air. If a dark spirit loomed out there to get his love, he'd have felt it. Wouldn't he?

He hadn't drunk any glow that morning and felt the effects. His powers weakened. He'd never *lose* his powers. Still, this side of the veil made them weak. He checked his belt and realized he hadn't taken any with him. Just as well. Most of what he had left would be needed in case of an emergency.

For now, his mind consumed him with thoughts of Brigit. First, her safety. He sped up to zig-zag through the streets, determined to get to her as fast as he could. People leaped out of his way as he cut a crosswalk.

Next, he thought about the dream she mentioned. That was a good sign. A wonderful sign, even! It meant that the Brigit from all those past lives might be awakening. He could only hope she would accept that. Could this Brigit deny her former self? What would that mean? Perhaps she could choose to stay in the mortal realm. What if she wanted to go back and live her life as a fairy goddess? What if she tired of that life, running from danger, and never succeeding?

He would have to tell her about the ritual. She would have to understand the stakes and would have to decide. Her hatred of magic and fairy tales daunted his hope.

"Oberon, help me," he whispered as he screeched to a halt outside her shop. "She has to remember, and she has to understand. Send your power to me now, please." He hadn't prayed in a long time. Maybe *he* lacked faith? "Please," he whispered again, kissing the triskelion around his neck.

He went inside.

"Brigit?" he called to her when he didn't see her inside. She came out of the back, just hanging up her phone. She ran to him, and he pulled her into his arms, squeezing her tightly to his chest.

"Sorry I hung up on you," she said. She didn't shake, though she was out of breath. "I called the police, and someone came out. He's back there now. Said it looks like some kids got in and wanted to play a prank."

Keeping one strong arm around her, they walked back to the mirror. The crack ran perfectly down the center. Each and every crease perfectly spidering out from the place the blade had hit - almost too exact. Magic. The hit had been guided and enchanted to create that image.

He wanted to command her to tell the officer to leave while his blood boiled and his heart burst with rage as he spotted the blade. A silver stiletto with a red cloth on the end: Arawn's trademark and his favorite way to mark his victims. It scared them, made them panic, and no doubt made their souls easier to harvest. He couldn't frighten Brigit.

The officer left quickly since there wasn't much he could do. He told her to invest in a security alarm and get a camera for the place, more if she could afford it. He gave her his card and told her to call if anything else happened and that he'd have a squad car patrol the area that night. Ildanach knew the mortal meant well, even if he just put himself in more danger than he realized. Humans always did. Ildanach had to stand by and watch events unfold. He could tell Brigit the truth. She could help.

"Thanks for coming." She stood on tiptoe to kiss his cheek. He was getting scruffy. "I guess it's nothing, like he said."

"No," Ildanach frowned. "It wasn't." He watched her face for a reaction, and she shrugged. Oh, her mortal indifference infuriated him! "Brigit, I have to tell you something." Nerves made his hands clench. He had to remind himself to breathe deeply since he panted when fear crept in. That didn't happen often.

"Uh-oh," she said lightly. "Here it comes. The big dark secret. Are you really wealthy because your father is a mob boss, and the junkyard is just a front for your illegal activities?"

"What? No." He ran his hands over the sides of his head. He could tell she caught onto his nervousness. He stood in front of her, his dark, mysterious eyes locked on hers. "I need you to listen with an open mind. I need you to pay attention and understand."

"Alright." She touched his face gently. "You can tell me anything. I'm pretty flexible when it comes to secrets, I think. I hope." She grinned encouragingly.

He silently appreciated her calm demeanor. She had become such a light in the last couple of days. She had really turned a corner in her life for the better, and her glow grew all the stronger for it. He prayed it didn't go out now.

"I'm not sure where to start. It's so important and a long story."

She shrugged. "Start at the beginning? I won't interrupt." She giggled and put her finger over her lips.

Ildanach frowned. "The beginning was...so very long ago, Brigit."

"Summarize," she suggested.

He sighed deeply. She was human. "Alright." His throat closed tight. He might lose her. What if she wasn't ready? What if she pushed him away and denied everything even more vehemently from this point on? Arawn was out of control, and there was nothing left except to try.

"Thousands of years ago," he began and saw her eyebrows

raise with confusion. "When the people of Europe still worshipped the spirits of nature, there was a large civil war among those deities. The darker spirits rose from their banishment in the underworld and came onto the human's earth where guardians were set to protect them. These guardians never yielded in their fight to protect the borders of the fairy realm and the human world, refusing love, a settled life, a family - everything. They were immortal, they didn't need such human comforts."

Brigit smiled. "And this is where it gets good, huh? One of them fell in love with a mortal?"

Ildanach shook his head and kissed her hand. "Worse. A goddess. This goddess loved him as well and knew their children would be more powerful than any living fairy creature. The spirits of the underworld couldn't allow their union. The immortals cannot experience love like humans do. To prove their love, the goddess took a human form and came to the mortal's side of the veil, following the guardian.

"When they came, they saw how mankind lost faith and turned to evil. The spirits of the underworld had come up and corrupted man, taking rule of them. The goddess knew a spell that would save the earth and cage the dark spirits and their leader. She and her love would have to commit the act of love on a sacred ground and vow to give up their fairy lives to seal the darkness away."

"Aw," Brigit sighed.

"It should have worked, but what the fairies didn't understand was the toll the mortal world took on them. On this side of the veil, the fairies were weak. They made a potion from their own essence and magic that would give them strength."

"Oh, I read that!"

A hint of relief came to Ildanach's eyes. Maybe she would believe him after all?

He went on, "The two lovers drank it and brought more of their kind over into the mortal realm, giving strength and company to the guardians. They were stronger for it and the dark spirits saw this. When word of what the lovers intended to do reached the leader and how the fairies were prepared to fight for the mortals who had abandoned them, he summoned hellish beasts and more dark spirits to his side. On a night of celebration for the mortals, he found them, tortured them, and stopped them."

"Oh." Brigit's eyes fell. "That's too bad."

"The evil spirit locked the guardian out of the veil, for they were already sworn to stay on this earth and protect the mortals. But the goddess..." His eyes glassed over as they watched Brigit. He was remembering, not just imagining. "He killed her."

"What? How?" she gasped.

"She had taken a mortal form to stop him. She was vulnerable and he, the guardian, wasn't there to save her."

"I'm sure he would have if he hadn't been locked away," she said quickly. She put her hand on his shoulder, trying to comfort and encourage him, as though he had been the perpetrator. If only she would believe.

"It's not over yet," he went on. "Every once in a while, every few lifetimes, the goddess is reborn, and the guardian finds her. And he falls in love with her."

Brigit smiled, happy to hear it. "And then they live together forever?"

She pulled back. Ildanach's eyes almost shone with tears.

"No," he said hoarsely. "Sometimes she dies of age, not knowing who she is. And he goes on. Repeatedly. Lifetime after lifetime."

She turned and took two steps back from him while he noted her tense posture. She crossed her arms, then uncrossed them and began pacing. She bit around her finger, looking away from him. Her eyes flashed with worry.

"I'm sorry," she said. "That story seems to have hit a nerve with me." She rubbed her arms. "Were the lovers first killed in a stone circle? Like Stonehenge?"

"Yes, Brigit!" He took her shoulders, focusing on her face. His eyes showed an intensity she didn't expect to find there. He waited for her to say something more, but she didn't. "Tell me you remember," he pleaded.

"What do you mean? I have no idea what you're talking about. There's this dream I've been having of the stone circle. It used to be vague, but ever since I met you, it's more intense. Last night was the worst. And... and, well, you were in it."

He read her discomfort, unable to ignore the signs. "Yes! Do you understand, my love? Do you know?" He took both her hands.

"Ildanach, you're scaring me," she whispered. He felt her begin pulling back.

"Think, Brigit. Outside of this life, there is another. And there is an afterlife as well. We can never be there if you don't remember!"

"We?" she coughed. "Ildanach, what are you talking about? Is this an analogy or something? You know I'm bad at this stuff."

"This is us!" he begged. "I am the guardian, and you are the goddess Brigit, giver of life! This," he grabbed up the silver stiletto, "is the weapon of Arawn, the dark spirit of the under-world, and he's come to take you once and for all. You do not believe in the world which you are from so he can take your soul easily now. If you are gone, how long will it be before another pair like us appears and challenges his reign? Or before you are born again? I do not know how much longer I can last alone."

"Ildanach, stop!" she screamed. She jerked away from him and put the register counter between them.

His heart broke to see her eyes brimming with angry tears. He had broken her trust.

"You're confusing me," she said, fighting to keep calm. "I knew you were strange when you first came in."

"And I knew you wanted more than this life to believe in," he countered.

"I don't!" she shouted. "I want the facts. I need a solid foundation. Not this fairytale shit! I thought that wasn't all you were. I can understand believing in it, like so many do. Or doing the practices because it ties you to something older, but this? Ildanach, I can't."

She dodged around saying outright that he was crazy. More than that, he could tell that he had broken her heart. She had believed in something. She had believed in him, and he had let her down. He had come into her life like a solid rock and he had crumbled, taking the footing from under her.

"Please, leave," she said softly.

So many words came to his mind to battle her doubts and prove himself, but his heart was too weak at the sight of her sorrow. Angry at his weakness, he nodded and left. If she wouldn't come with him now, he had to find and stop Arawn. No matter the cost.

Chapter 17

The Calm

Ildanach left quickly. He was well-versed in Arawn's style and knew if he wasn't hanging around now, he wouldn't be back for a while. He had motivation, but even he took his time. Fairies were old and did not rush like the mortals on this side of the veil. He had to get Robin's eyes and ears out on the street to find some information. The street fairies knew the movements of almost everyone just because they like gossip so much. The old side of town would be his best bet.

After he called Robin and had him begin, he did some searching of his own. He tried to focus on that task and put Brigit out of his mind just for an afternoon, but every word rang in his ears. She had been sweet, even flirty, and he used that to his advantage. Was it wrong to lure her in, only to turn around and try to convince her that she was a reincarnated goddess? Who would believe that?

I should have not said anything, he thought angrily as he made his way to the old downtown area. Maybe the council had not been wrong in their concern for him. Maybe he should enjoy this time with her and move on. Robin would tell him he enjoyed the pain every lifetime and needed to cut his addiction. He hoped each time he found her would be the last time. Hope was a fool's drug.

In an abandoned church near the playhouse, he ran into a gang of small trolls who were planning mischief for the highway bridges. Their love of bridges hadn't changed in the thousands of years he'd spent on this earth.

He approached the grey-skinned, humanoid-looking creatures, unbuttoning the top of his shirt to let his guardian talisman do the talking for him. From his hip, he took a large-barreled handgun loaded with quartz dust. For some reason, the trolls didn't like it, so he made sure to carry some when out hunting to ensure the peace.

"What do you want, fairy-trapper?" a scrawny troll sneered, popping the collar to a stolen, old leather jacket. "We're not breaking any rules. We're allowed mischief. Oberon said so himself."

"I know you don't bow to Oberon," Idanach said. "I'm not here to discuss politics. I need your ears and eyes."

"Oy!" shouted the little troll. "We may not be pixies, but we've not got water on our brains. You can't have 'em! No matter the price."

"Not literally, you stupid clay-glob." He took the quartz gun out, letting it hang in his hands. "You know the hounds, yes? You know Arawn?"

They nodded.

"Watch for him. And if you tell me where he is within twenty-four hours..." he stopped. What would a modern troll like in exchange for information? He hadn't dealt with them much, as they really were the most discreet of the magical races. "I'll get you a barrel of mead from that local brewery?" he said at last. He regretted the questioning tone he unintentionally put on it.

The troll crossed his leather-clad arms and drummed his fingers. "These are not the days of Arthur, guardian. I can get all the brew I want."

He looked around. The other trolls were dressed like the cast of Grease, some sitting in broken-down cars, the tops sawn off roughly.

"Motors!" Ildanach said quickly, smiling. "Foreign even. Ferrari."

The troll's eyes lit up a little.

"Audi RS 5?" he asked, smiling like a troll himself.

"You have this?" the troll said out of the side of his mouth, skeptical.

"In four colors," Ildanach whispered.

What had been just a small flickering behind the troll's eyes now blazed like a beacon; he practically licked his lips as he replied. "For that, oh green guardian, we'll follow even Arawn to his dark, undead halls!"

Ildanach smiled. "Good, because that's who you're tailing."

After that, he sat a moment on his bike. Brigit emerged in his mind's eye. He punched his metal tank in front of him angrily, bruising his knuckles. He could have handled telling her better. He could have told her differently. He needed her to love him. No, he wanted her to. Yearned for her to. It didn't even matter to him if she regained her memories or not. He loved this Brigit.

If he took it all back, said it wasn't true, and begged her forgiveness, maybe she'd love him. He could relinquish his immortality and stay with her. One last time with his love. He would die, pass on, and another guardian would rise. Eventually. He didn't know how long it took for another fairy guardian to arrive and didn't know what damage the rogue dark spirits could do in that time. Would it be hours? Would it be decades or centuries? The fairies took their time. It may be lifetimes before another guardian rose. And even then, a new guardian could not do what he could.

Brigit made the spell hundreds of years ago for her and Ildanach. They had to lie together, make a vow, and give up eternal life together in the throes of ultimate passion. No one else could perform this rite. The binding of Arawn would not be permanent. They had to sacrifice for only a moment of peace.

"Maybe I've done my part," he said. "Perhaps it is time for Ildanach, the warrior of ages, to pass on."

Then Brigit would be alone and what if her memories did come back, replacing what she knew now, erasing him? She would be alone. So alone, wondering what happened to him. Born over and over again. An eternity of loneliness.

"Ah!" he cried out, his heart and mind overcome with the anguishing thoughts. "Come on," he grunted. He couldn't lose it. Too much depended on him.

Focusing on safe-guarding the earth instead of his sorrow, Ildanach peeled out and raced to touch base with the fairies in the woods. The more people who knew about Arawn, the better. He'd hold off on talking about Brigit.

"I just thought something good would come," Brigit sniffed to Mary. She and her friend had gone out to clear her head and Brigit let herself be talked into a foot massage. "Like you said, you know?"

"Well, men are rats," Mary supplied. She didn't really know what had gone down; just that Brigit had showed up at her coffee shop crying about fairies and Ildanach. "I guess I shouldn't have egged you on. Too soon?"

"No, I just blew it. I blow everything. I don't know how to handle relationships, men, hardship, stress. I'm so bad at being a human." A fresh stream of tears trickled down her face. "I don't know anything about being in a relationship. Everything I know is from the movies. Should we be making out? Having sex already? I don't know."

The woman giving the massage looked a little awkward as she added her own attempt at help. "My husband left me for a man."

Mary and Brigit stared at her.

"At least you got out fast," Mary said to Brigit. "The police are watching your place, nothing was stolen, and you know what?"

"What?"

"That meditation class is still open if you want it. I need someone to do something in my loft if I want to keep it. Please, Brig? Just try it."

Brigit wiped her eyes. Maybe finding her own inner peace would help. Maybe showing others how to relax would help her. "Maybe I jumped on the find-a-man thing too fast."

"No," Mary smiled. "You are free as a bird and should do what you want."

"Ugh, sounds exhausting. I'd rather - I don't know - eat all day and watch TV."

Mary wrinkled her whole face at this. "Are you going to be one of those girls who eats when they're depressed?"

"If you don't, then you're lying to yourself and your fridge," she said simply, hiding a smile. Then she sighed. "He just felt right, you know? He was everything I wasn't. Everything I'm not."

"Aw, Brig, don't say that."

"He was. He was peaceful, happy, honest." She sighed and laid her head back. "Why can't I be those things?"

"Because you're human," Mary shrugged.

"Damn."

"Uh, I mean, he is too, of course." Mary slapped her forehead sarcastically. "Let's go check out my loft, yeah? Decorate it with your store. That way people can go over there and buy afterwards."

"Oh yeah, you'll be pleased." She dried her feet off. "I ordered books for the store. Some novels and other stuff. I don't know what I was thinking. I did get some on magical herbs and aromatherapy stuff. You think that will be good?"

"Yeah! Oh, Brig, that's awesome!" Mary hug-dived her and squeezed tight. "I can't wait to see what you do with the place."

They went to her store and Brigit grabbed boxes and boxes of left-over merchandise and spread it out in the cool, wide loft. The wood floor shined with polish and plenty of towering windows let natural light in. Assuming the clouds broke for once in their lives.

"I forgot how inspiring this place is," Brigit said, looking around. Yes, she needed to do this. She needed to keep Ildanach out of her head and do something else just for her. It was hard not to think of him, though. Every triskelion, every trinity, and magical crystal reminded her of him.

Was I wrong? she wondered. Did she leave him too fast? Maybe she caught him at a bad time. The morning seemed ages ago. She had been so tied up in the note and mysterious blade that the police had confiscated. There was a chance she hadn't behaved well.

"Stop," Mary said, nudging her friend with her foot. "I see you thinking about him. Concentrate here. This space is yours for a month. What goes where?"

Brigit picked up a large tapestry with Celtic symbols on it. "I only know this stuff, so it will be a Celtic themed meditation. The sabbats need to be indicated with little altars around the room to mimic the year wheel." She stood up and pointed as Mary marked each spot with a candle. "Samhain at twelve o'clock, Mabon here, Lughnasadh..." She stopped.

"What?" Mary asked, her arms still full of colored candles. "You have to have them all, right? I mean, you can't skip out on one."

Brigit chuckled mirthlessly and put her hands on her hips, shaking her head. "The god Lugh."

"Yeah, I know of him. I'm more into the Egyptian side, so what about him? Master of all abilities, sling-bearing adventurer. He was pretty cool in legend. You don't like his festival? Help me out, Brig, what's wrong with Lugh?"

"It's another name for Ildanach."

"Oh, shit." Mary quickly put the colored candle for Lughnasadh back into the box. "Maybe not sabbats? What about elements? We can do the five elements. Even though you don't believe in the spirit one."

Brigit nodded. "Yeah, let's do elements. We can all sit in the circle and each student can set up their mat in the element they feel best for them that day."

Dodged that bullet, she thought. She had forgotten about the festival for Lugh. Thinking back, she realized that Ildanach had come into her life very close to the festival celebrating the spirit of his namesake. She paused as a strange sensation creeped over her. Like when you learn a devastating truth for the first time. She thought back to the ridiculous story he had told her about fairies. Could he perhaps have been that spirit? Not named for him. Actually *be* him?

"Gods, I'm stupid!" she shrieked. "How can I think that?"

Mary took this opportunity to turn on her speakers. She had taken a relaxing Celtic mix from the box and let its soothing tones wash over them both. Then she turned on her oil burners, armed with lavender to calm Brigit down. That should help.

Soon, the loft twinkled in decorations like a temple from days past. Tapestries lined the walls, candles and potted ferns dotted the sides. With the lights dimmed and the music playing, it was almost like a fairy ring.

Brigit smiled. "Thanks, Mary, this is amazing." She breathed in the lavender and did a short exercise in her mind to release her stress. It helped a little. She exhaled. "I'll start as soon as I can. This will be great."

Chapter 18

Separated

The loft - or as Mary called it, the temple of calming pleasures - sat idle for almost two days when Brigit finally got in her order of books. She almost screamed with joy at receiving them because they dragged her attention away from the other thing - or rather two things - that had been plaguing her mind and making her cry in the early hours of morning.

The morning after setting up the "temple" Brigit had come down from her apartment to see her car parked out front. It looked like the accident had never happened and Ildanach had also fixed the automatic window on the driver's side of the car. It had been broken for almost a year and she hadn't been able to roll down the window because it never went back up.

Dreading a note, she hadn't gone inside the car for almost a day, only to be disappointed when she did and found none. He obeyed her wishes and stayed away. She had now been checking the mail, hoping to find a bill from the junkyard or something to indicate that she owed him. So far, none had come. If she wanted to pay for the fix, she'd have to go in.

"It kind of makes me angry," she said to Mary as she

unpacked the books. "I mean, I should be paying for that, right?"

Mary shrugged. She had kind of become Ildanach's defender over the last day, trying to get Brigit to not hate him. "He is still your friend. Brig," she adopted her very rare, serious tone, "you should call him. Don't you think?"

Brigit wanted to cry out with a huge yes. He had said some really crazy things, and she had no idea how to work around them. The worst part was the nagging feeling she had at the base of her skull that said he was telling the truth.

And worse still: she wanted him. A part of her she couldn't control screamed out for him. That part made her cry at night and had her checking her mail for a bill from him or jump at the sound of a motorcycle speeding by her shop. She prayed it would be him, even though neither she nor Mary had seen him for two days.

"Well, I better at least skim these so I know which ones to recommend to customers." Mary quietly left to open her coffee shop.

Brigit opened her store, but no one had come in yet. A strange delay in traffic always trickled through just before the holidays and Brigit never minded it. She took out a large stack of books and pushed Henry and his curious nose out of the way. The one on top looked strange, and she couldn't remember ordering it. That turned out to be the case with most of the books. She had ones on spells and magical herbs for the very devout and fairy meditation, something she'd never heard of before. Then there were more simple ones, like meditating to the sabbats and the witch's year, the cycles of the moon, and the most potent magical times. She had a few picture books and mythology anthologies thrown in for a diverse mix. She smiled, hoping she had covered a large base of interests.

Picking up one of the thicker ones, the first one she forgot she'd ordered, she flipped to the index and saw a list of spells by category. Household spells, spells for love, spells for good fortune and money - a large list. Then one of the last ones under "miscellaneous spells" caught her eye: a spell for better memory and recalling things you may have forgotten.

She checked to make sure no one browsed the store or lurked behind merchandise. Satisfied, she flipped to the page. The spell was invented by a woman from Kansas, it read, and she used it to remember assignments in school while in college. She talked about how she later perfected it to work for almost anything. A side note is what made Brigit act next: in a little box near the bottom of the page, it made a suggestion for calling up memories from a past life. That wasn't too weird for a spell book, right?

"Many of us are reincarnations," the passage read. *"Though not all hold this belief to be true, you can decide for yourself by using these simple methods to enhance the memory spell, provided you have a focus."*

"What am I doing?" Brigit asked a few moments later. She cast the circle and sat in the center with all the provisions around her. She was alone and Henry didn't try to stop her.

"Okay," she sighed. She read the phrase in the book, lit the candle, focused on the goddess Brigit and her dream. She chanted the strange phrase again. "Be light, be calm," she said at the end. "Open your mind, blah, blah."

She gasped! Before her eyes, a village appeared. An old one with thatched roofs like in the movie *Braveheart*. It looked like

Scotland, too. She closed her eyes. "No way this is happening." The smoke from the incense filled her nostrils.

This time, she saw the stones again. The figures danced just like in her dream. She snapped her eyes open, enhancing the clarity of the scene before her as though she were really there seeing it before her. She tried to speak, a giggle came from between her lips instead of words. She felt so happy, weightless with inner glee and her heart bursting with joy. She looked to the side.

Dark eyes, mysteriously framed by glossy, dark brown hair greeted her. His chin looked scruffy with stubble, intensifying his rugged, handsome look. His eyes sparkled with gladness. She knew those eyes. She wanted those eyes to watch her forever.

"We'll have eternity if we choose," he said. It was Ildanach's voice too. Light, deep, and playful. "Tonight is our night."

He leaned in and kissed her hard with his warm lips. She kissed him back, desperate to have him with her. She pulled him close, the urgency growing. She was so glad to have him back in her arms. He would take care of her; make sure she had no worries. And she would do the same for him.

The doorbell rang as a customer came in.

Brigit scrambled to her feet and greeted them with a warm smile. "What can I help you find today?"

"I need a salt lamp," the old woman said. She stopped. "Oh my, are you alright, miss?"

Brigit quickly put her hand to her face and realized tears drenched her cheeks. Her chest ached. She glared at the spell book. That was too real.

"If memories rise to the surface too easily, it is a genuine memory and may not be a past life, but something long forgotten or a secret wish," the passage said sweetly.

"Secret wish, my ass," Brigit growled. "Salt lamps are over here."

The day after Ildanach met with the troll, Robin had news. Grateful for the work, he listened as the sprite recounted the report.

"You must have just missed them," he said, scrolling through his phone. "A gang, glamored to look like bikers, in the forest. They've been causing some unrest. Using glow in public. Magic tricks. Not good stuff for those of us lying low."

"You're right," Ildanach nodded, oiling his saddle bags. "I would have seen them. Maybe we track them, see how they're hiding so well."

Robin bowed out and promised to keep an eye out while Ildanach distracted himself with tracking a biker gang. The texts he received from Robin throughout the day almost made him laugh: "Look for leather and tribal tattoos. Or follow the smell of gas." One even suggested he camp out at the roadhouse off the highway, since most faeries threw themselves into the parts they played. Ignoring the annoying sprite, he rode to the trail entrance of the woods and walked out on foot.

The woods near the city were often populated by more faerie life than the mortals realized. He found faerie rings, the prints of a faun, and even pixie dust laid out in distinct humanoid shape on a rock where a couple of tiny pixies had engaged in adult activities.

He snapped a picture and texted it to Robin. "You might consider this so you're not so tightly wound," he added to the image with some choice emoticons.

"Stop snooping in the woods and get to the roadhouse," Robin replied.

Curious and not finding anything suspicious, Ildanach rode several miles out of town the next day. The roadhouse in question had been the spot of migrating faeries a few times. Gas stations, rest stops, out of the way motels - all of these were favorites of fae on the move.

Ildanach went to the bar inside the NASCAR themed stop and ordered vodka neat. His eyes trained on individuals, looking for telltale signs of hidden fae folk. He expected to have to work harder, but this gang had no fear. Seven of them sat together, adding ample amounts of glow to their beverages before downing entire bottles in one go.

"How do they have so much?" he mused softly, trying to get a good angle to take a picture to send to Robin. "Why do they have so much?"

That question was soon answered when one of the waitresses saddled up to the table and flirted casually, touching one of the biker's long ponytail. Ildanach couldn't hear the conversation, but in just a few seconds, the girl discarded her tiny apron and left out the back with the biker. No doubt remained: these were the ones Robin had heard of. He'd need backup.

"Sounds like something I might try," Robin said over the phone while Ildanach watched them for a second night.

This gang showed just where their loyalties were. "Hounds of Hell biker gang?" Ildanach laughed. "As if no one would notice."

"No one would if they weren't looking," Robin replied. "Might die from the cringe though."

"They're moving!" Ildanach hissed when they readied to leave the roadhouse. "Call you later."

"Be careful," Robin said before hanging up.

He followed them out to the old hydro in the forest, which had become a common ground for druggies, alcoholics, kids skipping school, and the occasional group of fairies who ingested too much glow. Glow-drunk turned into a rarity now too and made the Hounds of Hell biker gang that much easier to spot with how they flaunted dumping it into their beer.

Ildanach parked his bike several yards out and crept quietly up to the hydro door. He carried everything with him that he thought he might need: stag gloves, coat, and plenty of iron blades to go around. He hoped he didn't have to use them. Then again, it had been centuries since he'd ran into minions of Arawn. They could tell him all he needed to know about Arawn's plans, if he persuaded them enough.

The door hung open a little and voices came from inside. Several chanted and one led them in a loud, commanding tone. Not a good sign. When fairies chanted, it meant something other-worldly was about to go down. Taking a chance, he peeked around the door to look inside.

Standing in a circle were the seven gang members and, in the middle, they trapped another fairy who looked to be of the messenger class. Just a sprite bringing information from one side to the other. This time, he got mixed up on the wrong side. From the torches and the large pewter symbols hanging from the seven fairies' necks, he assumed this to be an initiation.

That didn't make sense. Seven was the number. Eight didn't

have near the power. What were they going to use the other for? Maybe a spy to the fairy court? Whatever their plan, he couldn't let it happen. Taking his sling from his belt, he slipped in an iron stone. He kicked the doors in and let one fly at the group. Panicked, they scattered and all took out iron blades, swinging to face him. The one in the middle didn't, though. He looked confused and shaken at being interrupted.

"Pledge week is over, boys," Ildanach said. He focused on the one in the middle. "You know these guys aren't going to play nice with you, right? They need you for something more sinister. I don't know what though. They have seven; there can't be any more."

"Which is why he was bait," the leader sneered. "Really Ildanach, I expected better from you. Balor and Arawn speak so highly of you."

"Oh really, Sluagh?" Ildanach said, raising one eyebrow. He now recognized the dark fairy from years before. Sluagh enjoyed the company of what the Catholics would call wretched sinners. "I should be honored. Balor himself, huh?"

The eighth figure wavered and vanished. Ildanach's stomach dropped. He wasn't even real. They had laid a glamour trap. The seven saw his face fall and wicked sneers broke out on theirs.

"Arawn is out of town," Sluagh said simply. "He wants to make sure you don't go finding maidens you ought not to. You see, she's very close to finding herself."

He swallowed hard, realizing they were referring to Brigit.

Switching to a threatening stance, one foot behind the other, raising his fist in a threat, he took his eyes off the others just long enough. "I swear to your dark gods, Sluagh, if you touch her!"

Two of them ran at him and pounced. They grasped his arms and twisted his shoulders hard and fast. He cried out from the pain, dropping his slingshot. While these two held him, kicking his knees in the back so he fell to them, another removed his utility belt, rendering him almost powerless.

"Ildanach, my old friend," Sluagh cooed. "Don't make me hate you yet. We just need to make sure you understand the severity of the situation." He swung violently, making contact with Ildanach's jaw, sending him sprawling to the floor.

"Face me one-on-one, Sluagh, and let's see how you like that?" He spat blood out as his captors took his arms again and a handful of his shirt to raise his face to Sluagh.

"Well, I've never been the fair fighting sort," the dark fairy sighed. He picked up Ildanach's own iron blade and hummed with delight at the stag leather that bound the handle. "Clever. You know I've been wondering how you handle the tools of our desolation. Now I know. This is a rare animal." He signaled and they tore his coat and gloves off, tossing them into the fire. Ildanach struggled, panic weaving through him. He needed those for his work.

"Ever wondered what it's like to feel this?" Sluagh held the blade up to Ildanach's face. "You've pressed it to my skin a fair few times in our past."

With all his strength, he pressed the flat of the blade against Ildanach's neck. Pain seared through his flesh as it burned against the iron. He gritted his teeth and didn't let one anguished sound come from his lips. He shook with the pain and effort.

"So strong. No wonder she loves you." Again, Sluagh pressed the blade, this time to his exposed shoulder. Unsatisfied with Ildanach's control, he grimaced. "I can't take your life." He didn't sound pleased or angry about this. A hint of resentment trickled through his tone that Ildanach didn't understand.

"Chain him," Sluagh ordered.

"I could tear you all apart!" Ildanach growled.

"You won't though. How nice is that?" Sluagh said in a singsong voice. "Don't be so decent next time!"

Panting, they dragged Ildanach to a post where the group took turns berating him with punches and kicks, unleashing their anger.

"Wonder why it hurts so?" Sluagh laughed. He held up his own set of iron knuckles which Ildanach saw adorned each members' hands. "Lined with leather. That was a bitch to do, but so worth it."

"What is wrong with-"

"With us?" the dark fairy interrupted. "That fiery girl of yours is getting too close. We even sensed magic from her shop. Too close. We like our freedom on this side. If she comes back and you two," he smirked, "you know. Then we're banished *again*. What about my life, guardian? What about the things I've done?"

Ildanach found it hard, given his present situation, to think that Sluagh deserved anything less than a trip down to hell.

Sluagh twirled the iron blade in his hand, then let the point rest right under Ildanach's right eye. The iron hissed and bit his skin. Without being able to hold the pain in, a tear of anger and agony rolled from his eye and down his cheek.

"Now, now, don't cry," Sluagh cooed. He halted when he saw the look in Ildanach's eyes. No sadness showed there; only hellish fury, a threat. Sluagh hesitated. "Hurry up, men."

They locked an iron shackle to Ildanach's ankle, burning his skin yet again, the iron sucking his power and strength the longer it pressed against him. He tried to even his breaths, the element straining with each effort. Iron poisoned the faefolk, like kryptonite, only worse. He tried to show a brave facade, unable to stop the shaking from the contact with so much iron. His blood boiled under his skin.

The seven stood back, their work done. Ildanach tried to leap out at them, take them one last time. The chain went taut, holding him in place by his foot. His knees shook, but he stood tall.

"To ensure Arawn can find you more easily," Sluagh motioned one of his men forward who held a brand from a small metal garbage can where the fire smoldered with his coat inside. "Sadly, as you know, we cannot pinpoint our own kind. This rune should help."

He took the brand from the fire, grasped Ildanach's head, and pulled it back painfully. "Don't get lost now."

With a great force, he pressed the flaming brand onto the side of Ildanach's neck. This pain overtook him. A deep scream ripped from his throat as the iron and fire marred his skin deeper and more deadly than anything he had experienced before.

When Sluagh stepped back, Ildanach fell to his knees, unable to stand. If he ever met Sluagh again, whether in his world or on the other side of the veil, he would tear him apart with an iron blade. He made this silent vow as his strength waned. He saw the seven leaving and whispered thanks for their departure. He wanted to shout after them, to tell them he would find them, and they would pay for the havoc they brought to the mortals. He wanted to threaten them if they went after Brigit. For that, for her safety, he would destroy a myriad of fairies.

Feeling the iron's poison leak close to his heart, he pulled his phone out of his pocket and dialed. He had to make sure Brigit was alright. Arawn would be back in town soon, he had no doubt, and he would want to stop what he knew was happening. Somehow, Arawn had found out about Brigit, and he wanted her taken out.

"Robin," he panted into the phone, his own blood and sweat trickling into his mouth. "I made a mistake. I need you to bring my spare tools." His vision began to darken, his poisoned blood choking him. He groaned.

Before he passed out, he tried to imagine Brigit. This is what happened because they were separated. If he hadn't tried to convince her just yet, she'd be safe, and so would he. He should have waited. With his last thoughts, he berated himself for not waiting.

Chapter 19

The Vivid Past

"Breathe in to your lower back and hold it just a moment before releasing your stress on your breath. Relax the nape of your skull and let the energy flow out through your fingertips."

Brigit tried to do what she instructed her motley crew to practice. She hadn't been surprised when her first few classes had been filled with skinny girls with tattoos and weird piercings and older women with long white hair. She knew her crowd.

"Drop your shoulders and make sure your weight is evenly distributed through your trinity seat: your backside, and each of your legs." She tried to balance herself. She felt so heavy. The day before, she had called the junkyard. She had caved. Not being able to stand their distance, she reached out. Robin had answered.

"Um, Ildanach's sleeping," he had said. "Yeah, he's had a really tough last few days."

She pressed for more information, but the damned little

redhead was too loyal. He wouldn't budge, swearing Ildanach told him to let him rest. No doubt for the best. What would she say to him? Part of her wanted him back to apologize. After all, she had been rather harsh. The other part wanted him to say sorry, that he joked and that he'd be more serious from then on.

He had been so adamant.

"Come onto your back now," she sighed. "And open your mind. You've all memorized your chants, so let's get started."

The room filled with silent, female voices calling out to higher powers for peace. She tried to open her mind and thought of the chant from the spell book the other day. She let the foreign words vibrate in her chest as she hummed them. The little waterfall she installed trickled down, the sound dripping down her spine, relaxing her. The air hung warm in the loft. The candles made the glow calming and peaceful. Above her, she gazed at the tree of life tapestry she'd pinned there. Its branches all interlocking, creating a circle that never ended. Her mother had made this one. Across the top of the tree it read "As it is in heaven" and on the bottom that matched it, "So below on earth."

The ever-winding branches cast a trance over her. With her eyes, she followed one all the way around the tree and down into the underside. The same branch circled back up into the center of the tree. She traced the branches around and around with her eyes. They never stopped. Not until she chose to let her eyes rest on the trunk of the tree. She closed her eyes and focused on her chant again. Her breath became shallower. Soft music began to play behind her. Curious, she opened her eyes and saw not the tapestry above her, but actual branches.

Confused, she sat up. She was dreaming again, and she couldn't control herself.

Her dream-self giggled and leapt up, going deeper into the forest that suddenly engulfed her view. All around her were other women dressed in white with long, flowing hair. They were preparing for she didn't know what. In a clearing up ahead, she saw the familiar scene of dancing figures.

"They come!" shouted one of the women, pointing back into the dimming forest. Close behind came a group of men adorned like their god Cernnonus, antlers reaching up from their brows, tall and majestic. In the lead strode a familiar figure.

Ildanach stopped when he spied the women. His bare chest glistened in the moon light. His muscles were tight, and his chest heaved from the running. In his right hand, he held a rope and spear.

"I've found my prey," he called out. "Come, Brigit, shall we have a hunt?"

The other girls giggled and ran away into the clearing, the other hunters followed with silent feet, crouching like tigers. Brigit stood her ground and thrust her chin into the air.

"Will you have me, dear hunter? Can you catch me?"

She spun, laughing, and ran towards the firelight and the others. A futile effort, of course. Ildanach was built for running and hunting. And she, in her human form, was made for worship. Slender and shapely, she enticed all who looked on her, her full mane of fiery red hair moved in a wind only it could feel. Her eyes burned like coals.

She ran to the stone circle and hid behind one stone, calling out to Ildanach to chase. He suddenly appeared on the other side, slinging his rope around her and pulling her in. She screamed playfully and pushed against his toned body. She wanted him but pretended to be disgusted.

"You mortals are all animals!" Her wide smile betrayed her words. "Bind me, will you, fiend!"

"I do like their games though," Ildanach said, lowering his eyes to her like a hawk in a dive. He swooped down on her and stole a kiss, pushing her against the stone. She gasped when his hand went right to her breast, massaging her playfully. "Why do you get to wear these white robes and I must be exposed on these nights of festivities?" He slipped his hand under one strap and moved it slowly down her shoulder.

"Our chests are flesh of desire, yes?" She cocked an eyebrow, pressing herself into his hungry hands. "It is ours then to say when we give it to you."

Ildanach kissed her neck, working his way down. "You think you're so mysterious that way, goddess? How many times have we made love?"

"And yet you still wonder what I look like without it on. I seem to be in the right here." She tilted her head back, languishing in his soft kisses. "It has been nearly a century since I've made love to you, guardian." She stopped, her body relaxing back in thought.

Ildanach pulled away, aware of her sudden sadness. Around them, the frivolities continued. The mortals could not know who they were. Only fairies who took on mortal forms for the evening to join them would know.

Brigit sighed and looked up into her lover's dark eyes as they reflected the fire around them. "Why me, guardian? Why must I die again and again?"

"Because I must stay on this side," he said softly. His voice adopted a deep tone of sorrow. He rested his head against hers. "It is my duty. I am immortal here because I am a guardian."

"Then come with me," she begged. "Come back and leave this to someone else. You have lived your time here."

Ildanach shook his head. "There is one who evades me. Every year, this time of year, he shows himself and his black work is laid out for me to see. He toys with me, I think." He closed his eyes, blocking out images of times passed.

Brigit nodded. "I remember now. This mortal mind has not yet recaptured all of my lifetimes. I see this." She motioned to the stones, to the fire. "I have seen it. Always here." She frowned, an idea coming to mind. "Perhaps we should move? Go to another place to escape these dark spirits."

"I cannot," Ildanach said. "I will not leave the mortals at his mercy."

Brigit shook her head, taking Ildanach's face in her hands. "You are too brave, too loyal. It is on this earth I speak of. There is a new land in the west. We can go there. A young people, just starting out with this new civilization they are so keen on. We can go and lead people to follow the old ways and keep your power alive." When he didn't reply, she added, "Please, my love. For us."

She knew Ildanach would not do anything that would endanger his people or the mortals he loved so much. Going to this new world would not be abandoning them. It would be creating a new following. Spreading the fairies over more land and giving hope and magic to more people. He had to see it her way.

"Time is moving faster these days," he said at last. "I only just thought it was the Renaissance. Our people were powerful then."

"That was nearly two centuries ago." Brigit smiled. "These people in the west need us. We need it. If we are far enough away, we can perform the spell and bind the dark ones for a time. Until..." she stopped and let her eyes fall to their earth.

"Until you die again," he finished.

"You are strong, my love. For staying each time."

"Not strong enough." He turned his face away, not wanting her to see him weak.

Brigit swallowed and tried to rekindle their touch. She slipped a finger on each hand into his belt and pulled his hips to hers. "You mean we have not given ourselves up to mortal life. To bind the dark ones?"

"I will not have any of your lives be the last," he said forcefully. "Who is to say what will happen once we die. Die for eternity!"

She stopped his mouth with a kiss and pulled his hand between her thighs. "I cannot speak of this now."

He reached down and cupped her face in his strong hand. He kissed her long and deeply. They would sail west, and they would try as best they could to start a new life and a new following.

The dream wavered for Brigit. She saw bits then, her mind fighting to return her to the present day. The journey her past life took proved difficult, though. For as long as Brigit remained on the mortal side of the veil, the more glow she had to consume. The voyage was the hardest on her, as none could be found on the ship. Fairies did not seem to be fond of the wide ocean that separated them and the great, unknown, western world. She wanted many times to leave the mortals and return to the right side of the veil, but Ildanach would not leave. If she left him now, she may never find him again, and so she stayed. She suffered illnesses, never achieving her immortality on this side as he did. It was not her place as it was his.

When they reached the west, they were surprised to find other spirits there in the shapes of animals. A different kind of fairy, still deities nonetheless. With their help, they were able to create a home like the other mortals. When this was finished, and they thought they were completely alone, Ildanach prepared to consent to the vow and to lie with her, binding the dark spirits until her death.

Chapter 20

Summon The Goddess

Brigit looked out over the vast plains of the west as the storms rolled in. That storm would be the deciding factor, she knew. She spent days in the company of the animal fairies of this strange new land and learned of the growth and conquering of it over many years. She heard of its hardships and how the people had kept their beliefs and ways alive. She admired it.

Her life flashed before her eyes, and she couldn't stop it. The clouds drew in and the rain poured down. Behind her, she heard the screaming lament of some of her sisters in the old ways. Many of her people were being accused and killed for their work with magic, and she did not have the power to stop it.

Ildanach went out to hunt a black stag at last. She didn't know there were any in the western world; he said he spotted one and she knew the power in the hide. He had also thought to find more fairies from their part of the world, to try to help with the situation, no matter how few of them there might be. The one tribe they had found didn't want to meddle in the affairs of humans. She began to understand.

"Death and death," a deep voice said in her ear. A shiver ran down her spine and back up to her skull. She should have known. She was alone. When else would a coward like Arawn strike?

"Death comes and so do you," she said through her teeth. The icy rain made her shiver, though this hate was for him. "And so I run, thus you follow."

Arawn sat enthroned on his grey horse, clothed in his grey robes of the underworld. In this time, he was not old as she knew him later. His pale face was smooth, alabaster flesh over sharp cheek bones. A green hue of stolen souls glowed in his eyes. He wore his white hair in a single braid over his skull and down his back, the sides closely shaven. "I came to see my work," he said in a deep, echoing voice. Every soul he'd consumed spoke with him, but in agony.

"Well done," she hissed. She looked around. There was no one in sight who would help her. None could see Arawn and would think her a mad witch like the others. She couldn't say more; she knew what he wanted. It was time to stop her before she and Ildanach could make the oath.

"What stays your rite, goddess?" he asked simply. "Is it that you know you will perish once you commit this vow? You delay too long."

"You know I am mortal now," she spat. "You have killed me before. What took you so long to find me?"

"Yes, yes, you could live years without the oath. Far longer than I have delayed this one time." He waved his pale hand. "With it comes the sacrifice of unnatural age. You will die at the rate a normal mortal would. Isn't that sad? Wouldn't it be better if you lived longer after the oath to keep me chained longer?" He leapt from his horse with a splash of mud.

Brigit gasped and stepped back.

Arawn went on. "If you perform this rite, I am bound. Only as long as you live. You give up immortality. Do you see the madness?"

Not now, she begged in her mind. Where was Ildanach? His hunt for a remedy for the mortals would be the death of her!

"You are a subject to the gods and goddesses," she said in an attempt to perhaps delay him with allegiance, "those of which I am nearly greatest."

"And yet you give that up to come and live on this side of the veil." He shook his head, an evil curl in his lip. "Why, why, oh goddess of life and healing?"

"To keep you and your kind at bay!" She screamed the words and lashed out with a blade she kept hidden under her long, full sleeves.

Arawn dodged, only just jolting to safety. The blade cut across his chest, ripping his grey robes and drawing out dark, purple blood. His eyes bulged with hate and anger at being taken by surprise, and that the attack came from one of his own.

"Devil woman," he spat. "You know nothing of my life and the horrors I have suffered!"

"I care not. Come take me, coward!" she screamed.

Instead, Arawn held out both of his hands, palms to her, and hissed in the old language. Behind him, a white, smoky portal tore the fabric of the mortal world and two white hounds with red ears emerged, teeth bared.

"Run, goddess," he whispered.

Panicking, Brigit bolted from the trio, knowing she could not fight them. She tried not to stumble as she ran through the uneven prairie and took a small, round bottle of glow from her belt. It would hardly work with her since she became a mortal being, though it did give her a little strength. The liquid ran down her throat like hot needles and into her stomach. She cringed, accepting the pain, taking the power. It gave her just a bit more speed.

Despite the glow, she could not move fast enough. This was one of the many, many times she had been hunted down by the hell hounds. As she ran, all of her memories came back. She saw herself die again and again. Her fear of death stopped her every time from completing the rite with Ildanach. The times she did allow herself to die made her pain ease. *Give up and die one last time,* she always told herself. Neither she nor Ildanach had ever given up. They always waited just too long.

A hound snapped at her ankle and the second pounced on her back, tearing into her neck with sharp teeth. She screamed, focusing on the past. The more distant past. Ildanach was there, pushing her hair behind one ear, and smiling down at her as though he had no other treasure in the world greater than she. The sun began to rise, casting warm light and a glow over them both.

"Better than last time," he whispered.

"Ildanach!" she screamed, as she fought the hounds off until the last. When would she not need to be saved? When would she make the choice to put this eternal death behind her forever? Why was it her choice? Why could she not be forced to?

"Brigit!" a familiar voice screamed over the planes in an unfamiliar way.

As red, mortal blood covered her eyes, she saw the form of

her love, her strong hero, charging down the dark spirit with a great, iron sword.

"**B**rigit, damn it, wake up!"
Mary's voice jarred her. Relief at the sound of her friend's voice flooded Brigit so much, it poured out of her eyes in hot, happy tears.

"Oh Ra, Mary, you would not believe the dream I had!" She grasped her friend tight, convinced she would never let her go. She held Mary like this and let a few rattling sobs escape her before she realized she was not bleeding from bite wounds all over her body. Everything blazed white, and a quick beeping told her that her heart raced.

She looked around at the glass door and the shaded windows. "Hospital?" she asked. Her hand suddenly went to the back of her neck. Nope, no dog bites.

"Yeah, you passed out in the class," Mary explained. Her own eyes flushed red, swollen. "About twenty-four hours ago, mind you. You've been out. Everyone thought you had fallen asleep, then you started to sweat and mumble." She wiped her eyes. "You had a seizure or something."

The dream. And that damned spell book. She had heard scary stories about people who meddled in magic and weren't prepared for the consequences. And now she was one of them. *Never again*, she swore silently. Not so much as a magical herb would pass her lips. Maybe the time had come to sell the store. A drastic step, but one she might have to take to maintain her sanity.

"I'm so sorry, Mary. It won't happen again."

Mary nodded, patting her shoulder. "So, you want to continue?"

"For now," Brigid shrugged. "I have people counting on me. They really liked it and I think I know what drove me over the edge." She didn't want to tell Mary, but she wanted to reassure her friend it was alright. "Not again. Ever."

Mary scrutinized her cautiously. "There's something else too."

Yes, magic had kicked her ass. Or something like it. She didn't want to say that out loud. She hoped it wasn't true, and that she had just gone into a trance.

"Please tell me Henry didn't escape while I was out!" Brigit gasped suddenly.

"No." Mary laughed and shook her head. "I'm glad that's what you thought of. You see, while you were out, you called out a name. In several varieties. Some were in panic, some were sad, and some were..." She pursed her lips and raised her eyebrows. "You know, a little, uh, passionate."

Brigit's heart tightened and then sunk. "Oh."

"And I also wanted you to know that he's outside."

"What?" she shrieked in a strangled cry.

What had sunk her heart just moments ago made it implode and lighten faster than she thought possible. He came. To see her. He had heard she was in trouble and had come! When was the last time that had happened?

She shook her head and rubbed her temples. How could he have ever been there for her when she had only just met him weeks ago? Crazy thoughts.

"I guess he'll come in then and see me all hospitalized," she said, smoothing the wrinkles out of her sheets. "Maybe that will turn him off."

"I can make him leave," Mary offered simply.

"No, it's okay. I'd like to see him. Clear some things up, you know?"

Mary didn't look convinced, resigned herself to her friend's wishes. She got up and left to get him, and Brigit waited. She clasped her hands in front of her and then put them under the blanket. Then she smoothed her hair and hoped nothing stuck in her teeth. Trying to calm her mind and relieve the demons from the dream, she gazed out the window. Dim grey coated everything, like an early snow would set in.

She heard heavy, booted footfalls enter the room. She wanted to look, hesitating and not trusting herself. What if she relapsed and wanted him back? Unable to stand it, she turned to face him.

He seated himself next to her bed, his tall, strong frame taking up most of her vision. His hair hung a little ragged, still glossy and shining. Where there had once been playfulness and sarcasm in his eyes, now caution and a mysterious darkness blinked in and out. She bet she looked pathetic, staring up at him, sad and hurt. She tried to put on a brave face.

"You never called," she said at last. Why let him get the first word?

"You told me to get out," he replied.

Did a hint of his usual sarcasm and cheek come through?

"I wanted to call, but I was afraid you'd get angry," he finished.

"Afraid of me?" she scoffed. Oh, her insides hurt! She wanted to take him into her arms, press his head to her and say she didn't care! She wanted to love him and willed herself to overlook the faults. It was never that simple. "And I thought you were the kind of guy to put in a little effort for a girl."

He smiled weakly and avoided her gaze, looking instead to the floor.

"What have you been doing, then? You would have called otherwise." She tried not to sound demanding, but knew she did anyway.

Now he really avoided her eyes. She sensed before he even spoke that he would not answer, afraid of hurting her, she realized. She wanted to say that nothing he could think up would hurt her. Even if she'd be wrong.

"Just been busy with shop stuff. Family matters," he tacked on quickly.

She did hurt. He had lied. Why would he lie to her? Why avoid telling her why he hadn't dropped a word?

"Ildanach," she said quietly, "Why won't you tell me the truth?"

Now he met her eyes. So, he hadn't fooled her. Of course not. "Would you believe something else?" he asked.

"Like what? Please, no more magic," she begged. Not that again. She grew sick to death of it. It had caused her to pass out and now she had a million horrendous images of her own death in her mind. Thousands of years' worth of torment boiled up inside of her, and it wasn't even real. How would she ever get rid of the feeling of dread? The torment of seeing those deaths? She prayed loving Ildanach would not be part of that. The memories she had with him were worth the fear from the others.

"Would you believe something you cannot right now?" He inched forward in the seat, wanting to be near her. Something in her eyes gave him hope. His hand almost reached out for hers and she almost responded.

She put on her brave face. "If I can't believe it, then no."

She saw the light drain from his face just before he masked it into an emotionless facade. He was being brave. She didn't want him to be brave. She wanted him to tell her what had happened, explain everything, even the things he couldn't possibly know about. She just wanted him to stay. He had tried, and that made her love him all the more. She shut him down again.

He stood up and leaned in towards her, then stopped. A beat later, he pulled back.

"I'm glad you're alright, Brigit." He tucked his long hair behind one ear and gazed down at her with unabashed longing. It warmed her heart and made her squirm under his eyes. "May I call on you tomorrow?"

"Yes," she said too quickly to hide any false apprehension. Mary would chide her for that later. "Um, I mean, yeah, if you want."

She tried to back out too late, the secret was out. Ildanach tried not to smile too, his perfect lips rounded at the corners just enough to show a smile. He turned to leave.

"Wait, please," she called. He stopped. She clenched her fists. "I'd like to try something."

He came back to her and knelt by her bed like a knight waiting to be bestowed an honor. "Yes?"

She swallowed hard and took a deep breath. Her thighs tingled as she put one hand on the side of his face and pushed his hair back the way he did to her. It was a very sexy look on him and made her smile. He replied by nuzzling his face into her hand ever so slightly.

"Okay," she sighed. She leaned in, closed her eyes, and kissed him.

Her mind exploded with joy and memories of kissing him flooded her mind. She loved taking his head in her hands this way - she always had. Her breath caught and picked up, her chest heaving as she put her other hand to his face, pulling him into her more.

She stopped. Bending her head down, she steadied her breath. She had seen what she wanted. She loved him still, and he loved her. He just wasn't going to force her.

"Call me and tell me how that felt," she said.

He stood. "Only if I can be honest."

A tiny weight dropped into her stomach. "Okay. Honest. Tomorrow."

Chapter 21

His Dark Past

Ildanach had closed the yard for days now. Ever since his run-in with Sluagh and the gang. He was in no mood to deal with customers, even though he had no stronger desire than to help mortals with their menial needs. Robin had been very understanding, though he took to disappearing for hours each day out of boredom. He tried not to bother the sprite over his vanishing as he knew he could be very overbearing at times, and Robin needed his freedom.

He watched his eyes in his own mirror as he lifted the weights he kept in his closet. Sometimes the bigger monsters were harder to take down and physical force became necessary. He hadn't been hunting in days, though. He checked on the ghost boy only to find him still roaming the halls, crying and looking for peace. Arawn would see to it that no one found peace. That's how he punished Ildanach. He would torment the mortals he loved until he gave up. Or, if he could raise enough souls, create an army of darkness to overtake. If that happened, Ildanach knew he would have to flee behind the veil and leave his mess for another guardian to clean up. That's how he became one.

Before the humans kept calendars, Ildanach had been a fairy warrior for the court. He mentored many fairies and had fought in many battles. Remembering the fairy court brought a longing to his heart. It had been years since he'd seen the other side of the veil, and the weakest part of him longed for that place again. The stronger part that yearned for Brigit.

He stopped and inspected his scars in the mirror. He healed fast and thanks to the glow, his powers were strengthened. He went to his nightstand to get one last sip of the wonderful stuff and found the round vile empty, glittering with residue. Frowning, he thought back, trying to remember if he had used it all. No, he had at least a swallow left. He remembered planning that out as there were some werewolves causing problems in Cincinnati that he had to take care of. He'd wanted the long road trip, however now with Brigit willing to listen, he'd have to cancel. Still, the glow was missing.

The thought of Brigit made him numbly pump the weights again. Something happened to her that made her think she could listen. He didn't know what transpired in her life to make her change her mind. He thanked the stars for it. No matter the outcome, he loved her. If he had to, he would give up his immortal life just to spend one last lifetime with her. With this new Brigit. She would never know the lives they had had together. She would never understand what it meant for him to touch her soft skin. She would never know how much she had loved running her fingers through his hair while he arched into her touch, touching her in return.

He longed to touch her like he used to. Their first touch was so long ago, yet vivid in his mind. He wanted to remember it, to watch the memory in his mind, but the pain painted a black hue over the memory. She, a goddess, had chosen him. Deigned to love him.

He pushed the weight above him harder, faster. How could he live a normal life? For her. It required the ultimate sacrifice. There was no other way. Or was there? He could wait for his Brigit to grow old and die. He'd watch from a distance, his love sinking into age, alone. He could wait again. For what? A more favorable version of her? Disgusted at the thought, he roared, throwing the massive weights across the room, lodging the bar into the wall. Plaster crumbled away and the next room came into view through the new hole. Clearing the anger that blinded his eyes, he saw Robin lying on the floor in the next room.

"Robin?" he called, a mild panic in his voice. Had Sluagh gotten to him? "Robin!"

He rushed out to his loyal companion. The imp's long red hair dripped with sweat, matted, and he shook. A strange glint shimmered in his sweat as it hit the sun. Ildanach recognized it at once. He had learned the hard way that a fairy on this side of the veil could overdose on glow. Never again.

"Robin, my vile little friend, what have you done?" He lifted the little sprite up and took him to the kitchen. Sitting him up in a chair, he steadied him before getting a cold cloth and a silver spoon. "Stay here," he instructed, to which Robin replied with a moan.

Secretly, in the top of his closet wrapped in black cloth, he kept a tiny vial of powdered iron. After his first scrape with overdosing on glow, Ildanach made sure to keep a way out near him at all times. He trusted himself to never do it again, even though his life was long, and he couldn't be sure something wouldn't make him do it again.

Back in the kitchen. He expertly dodged around his mountain of dirty dishes to get a glass of water and sprinkle some iron into it. He stirred the concoction with the silver spoon, then propped Robin's head up.

"I cannot pretend this will not be the most vile, disgusting thing you've ever had to endure," he sighed. "For us, it seems ten times worse. Don't spit."

Ildanach tipped the glass, dribbling the liquid down Robin's throat. When the sprite coughed and tried to spit out the fairy poison, Ildanach put his hand over his mouth, apologizing again. He had never wanted to harm Robin, but only iron could negate the amount of glow he had ingested. Stupid sprite. Too much glow was poison enough. He had to understand that iron would help just this once.

He waited a few moments, his hand on Robin's shoulder, letting him know he hadn't left. It would take a while for the iron to have its effect and the results were never pretty. Ildanach left him for just a moment to fetch an old bucket and another wet cloth. Just when he got back, Robin gagged and lurched forward, spilling the contents of his stomach into the bucket.

"Oh, breakfast never looks good the second time around," Ildanach said lightly, patting Robin's back.

"Your breakfast is never good," Robin moaned, finally speaking. "That's why I always want something from a shop. Powdered donuts would be good."

"Gross." Ildanach ruffled Robin's messy hair. He set the bucket outside to clean later and then sat across from his friend. He crossed his arms, the muscles hard from his workout making him that much more intimidating to the little sprite. "So?"

"What?" Robin snapped back. "You wouldn't care. You've been too wrapped up in moping a thinking about that shop keeper."

Ildanach didn't roar back. He didn't rage about his life and his sorrows. His eyebrows tensed in sad understanding.

"I know," he breathed quietly. "I'm sorry. I should focus, perhaps. If I had not been so selfish, I would not have driven her away or let you go."

Robin frowned. "Drove her away?"

Now he let his guard down. He uncrossed his arms and leaned onto his elbows, running his hand through his hair with a sigh. "I let you down, Robin Goodfellow. You are a much better fairy than I. You stay by me, do your work.... You are good." A small attempt at a smile eased the tension in his face. "I am sorry I had to poison you. That will take hours to get over. Still, I cannot help the way I feel. I have let her down again. And this," he waved his hand to Robin, "reminds me of the worst time."

When he said this, Robin knew a dark story lurked behind the words. "Tell me," he said. "I need a good story while I recover."

Ildanach shook his head. "I don't think I can tell it."

"Then let me use a trick Oberon taught me." Robin leaned in and his green eyes turned solid, his pupils gone, and they glowed bright even in the light. "Let me see it. Herne hates I can do this just as well as he."

Ildanach felt Robin's power touch his mind, looking for his

story. "Have you ever read my thoughts?" he asked suddenly. "Why did you not tell me you could do this?"

"Because then you'd be paranoid and you're already a classic over-thinker. Can you imagine how fast you'd kick me out?" Robin asked simply, something of his old, impish self showing through his illness. "And no. I swore to you that I'd never go against your will."

"Then let me show you." Ildanach relaxed and brought the painful memory up to the front of his mind. "It was the first time... I saw her die."

Torrential rain poured over the scene of iron-colored mountains, an ocean of waving grass, and a tall, rectangular castle. Its primitive walls were guarded by fire, archers, and bearded men in robes. These last were acolytes of the fairies, mortal learners of their ways, who in turn instructed followers and worshippers of the goddess and her realm. Their eyes trained on the moon-lit horizon, waiting with tense brows.

Ildanach stood guard in the king's hall, at the right hand of the throne. His blade unsheathed and his armor already bloodied.

"The invasion has started, my king," an acolyte said. "The enemy comes with dark forces I do not know."

"Arawn," Ildanach said sharply, disgust on his every feature. "The one who killed Prince Pwyll. The guardian before me."

"Can you stop him?" the king asked of his fairy guardian.

Ildanach wasn't sure, he couldn't bring himself to tell the

mortals the truth. "Your daughter marries the northern king, yes?"

The king nodded.

"Then make it now rather than on the morrow. Time is short. I will try to stop the dark spirits, but you must follow through as well, no matter what happens."

The mortal king nodded, thankful to have someone so powerful by his side. "Thank you, warrior."

Ildanach left the hall. He had one thing to do before going out to face the murderer of the last guardian, Prince Pwyll, and facing a threat he couldn't begin to imagine.

He took the stone steps two at a time with his long legs to make it outside and to the little garden where prayers were said to the fairies. Underneath a willow tree stood a simple stone well that the priestesses of the goddess used to scry to the fairy world. He didn't know what the fairies allowed them to see. It couldn't only be useless glances.

"Brigit," he called to the well, "My goddess, my love, answer me!"

"Danger!" the well shouted back in many voices. "Brigit has gone from this world. See her here."

The well rippled and lit from beneath the waters. As though reflected there in the rippling water, Ildanach saw Brigit bound to a stone table, a host of grey spirits around her, white hounds, and ghostly horses.

"How?" he roared into the well, knowing it would not answer.

Fury fueled his gait as he dashed from the garden to his horse in the stables. In his saddlebags, he had all he would need.

He took the bags and upturned them, spilling everything out and tossing irrelevant items aside.

"Master?" yawned a bleary-eyed Robin. "What are you looking for?"

"The glow, all of it. I need it." His voice scratched, husky and wolfish, a growl in every word. "Ah!" he hissed after touching an iron blade. "Have you not yet found the black stag, wretch? I need the hide for my iron weapons."

Robin frowned, offended. "No."

"Then I need it all." Ildanach took every little round bottle he had and dashed out just as fast as he'd entered, leaving the mess.

He threw back bottle after bottle, leaving a glass trail of glowing purple behind him. He felt it right away. First, the surge went to his fingertips. Then it weakened his legs, making them blocks of lead as he tried to trudge along. He took the iron blade from his belt, his hand burning and the pain searing through his vision. Everything started to glow with a purple haze.

"No," he moaned, falling onto the wet ground. "You bastard!" he screamed to himself. "What have I done?"

His chest constricted and he couldn't breathe. His head seared, like his scalp erupted in fire. All around him, he could hear every thought of every being. He felt their every emotion and could suddenly bend them to his will. He had no control.

"What is this?" he gasped. "Brigit!" he called out, hoping she could hear him with his amplified powers.

And he did see her. She looked up, as though spotting him amongst the stars. She lay tied down, looking to him for help. A sharp blade slashed across her throat. Her eyes widened and her lips parted gently in surprise.

"I wanted you to save me," she whispered with her dying breath.

With the last of his sanity, Ildanach screamed into the night, a roaring wail that sent birds from their perches and foxes from their dens. If he had not cared so much about the mortal's war, he would not have lost her for the first time. If he had not thought that the only way to save her was the power of the glow, then her warm blood would not be mingling with the cold rain.

Robin winced, closing his eyes tightly, a tear dripping down his sharp cheekbone. "I'd forgotten about that battle." He tried to laugh. "I remember now. That was just after Oberon had me exiled. Took everything I owned. Literally." He shook his head at the memory. "You cannot blame yourself, Ildanach. She did not fight back."

"Because she trusted I would be there for her." His eyes were hard, dark, and distant. "At the first test of faithfulness, I betrayed her. I don't know what she thought the next time we met." He clenched his fist, his veins standing out. "Why can I not save her? I can never save her!"

Robin got up to go into his room and lay down. "You know the answer to that."

Yes, he knew. Would he have the courage to give up his life forever? He thought he had the courage to save Brigit, that was obvious. A Brigit who knew nothing about their lives together?

The desire for her and the fear of death tore his heart into pieces. The pain alone was enough to kill him.

Chapter 22

Behind The Veil

Brigit leaned her head against the cold, glass front door. The rain outside made her headache worse somehow. It was almost noon and Ildanach hadn't shown up. Maybe something had happened. Maybe he ran off being crazy, pretending to fight goblins and spirits. Mary had suggested that he might be one of those Live Action Role Players who took their board games way too seriously. Brigit had put aside the idea. He radiated too much honesty and spoke too level-headedly to let a game get the better of him. He was strong and smart, and everything she thought she could never be.

That story he told about the goddess and the guardian still rang in her head, even though it had been so long ago. She had tried not to think about the dreams she'd been having that matched his story almost perfectly. And the glowing yoga instructor bobbed in and out of her mind every time her brain calmed down. And her passing out in her meditation class. Those visions had been so vivid, she swore she could remember what happened next. They weren't in her head like dreams;

they were solid, like memories. She *knew* what was going to happen.

She called Mary to talk while she waited. "I remember when he left me that day on the plains," she said. "I was angry at him the first time, but so pleased he'd found the stag. He needed to find it. So, I let him go. I think part of me knew that the death fairy would be there. I knew." She rubbed her forehead. "Why did I know and not care?"

Mary sighed on the other side. "Remember, Brig, this wasn't you. This was some crazy dream you had because of the warmth and incense and who knows what else. Were you...drinking or...?"

"No, Mar, I don't drink that often." She put her hand into the soft, hot roll that was Henry in his hammock. He jerked awake, glaring at her for putting her cold hand into his cage. She stroked his little head and he yawned. "I know it sounds crazy. I can't shake the feeling. It was so real."

"Remember back in high school, when I told you I lost my virginity?"

"Yeah, you teased me for weeks after," she said through gritted teeth.

"That was a dream. I totally thought it was real."

"What? You kept that from me all this time!" She smiled a little. Of course. Mary had been the student librarian for their high school. She should have known.

"Well, there you have it. So, I need to go. I'll see you after you talk to him, okay? Call me and we'll get together right away. I'll bring wine."

Brigit rolled her eyes. "Okay. Thanks."

Lightning flashed. In the sudden, bright blue light, she saw the outline of a man heading towards her store. She hadn't seen him approach from the sidewalk and jumped when he came through the door, the wind howling behind him. The sudden entrance shocked Henry too and he tumbled out of his hammock, shaking his whole body angrily, his bell-collar tingling.

The man shook his umbrella off out the door then closed it. "Sorry about the wind, I didn't know it was so strong," he said. He had one of those deep, smooth voices you'd expect to hear on some audiobook about the history of Vikings or some other deep, rumbling narration. Dark, commanding tones came from a cavernous chest. In the flash of lightning, she swore a mask of the younger, imposing fairy of death lit across his face.

Brigit rubbed her hands, shaking off the spell of his voice. "What can I help you find today?"

"I've actually come to see you." He made his face friendly. "I'm a Seer of sorts and I thought you might be interested."

She snorted and shook her head. "You're barking up the wrong tree, sorry. I don't do that stuff. I don't believe in destiny, set futures, or anything."

The man nodded, understanding, but took a step towards her anyway. "Then why do you carry a spark of hope inside you, Brigit?"

She started, frowning. "How do you know my name? Do I know you?"

He shook his head. "I know you. I know the sorrows you've been carrying, the hardships no one understands. You try to tell people, like that little friend of yours across the street, but she just can't understand. She can't. She doesn't know what you've been through and never will because she's not you."

She caught herself focusing on his voice again. So low and smooth. Soothing, almost. His hair gleamed white and shiny, glowing in the soft light of the many lanterns in the store. He had a kind face. She noticed a talisman around his neck, mostly because she thought it too glowed a soft golden. A yellow gem in the likeness of a globe with a silver crack ran down the center. It resembled Ildanach's in so many ways. She smiled, thinking of him.

"I'd like to think I try though," she said in her own defense. "I mean, I know Mary will never really understand. Still, she's so good to me. And I work hard at life."

"Do you?" he said slowly. "Really? You sit in this shop day after day, wishing you could get out, go on, move to a new life. Something passionate, exciting, fantastic."

"Everyone wishes," she said.

"Not as hard as you."

She shrugged. "I don't know. I don't know anything, really." She rubbed her eyes, beginning to feel groggy and relaxed all at the same time.

"I know what you want," he said lightly. "Shall I tell you?"

"Go for it." She had nothing else to do. This guy claimed to be a fortune teller, why not let him try? She knew all the tricks anyway. How they looked for clues about her from their surroundings and what she wore.

"You are sad," he started. "All that I said before, you want. Beyond that, and beyond your strong, independent facade, you want a man in your life to take care of you."

"Hey," she interjected, "everyone needs companionship. I'm fine on my own."

"You are," he nodded. "And that disturbs you. Why are you so confident, you ask yourself?"

"Because I have to be!"

"Why? Why do you have to be so strong, so alone? What have you done?"

"I ignored my family, okay? I pushed them away to show them I was fine. To show them that I could do it."

"And you did! Here you are." He spread his arms wide, showing the store. "Alone, and fine. Why are you alone, Brigit?"

She nearly glared now, her eyes getting moist. What was this guy trying to do? Get her to cry? Get her to admit she thought she was responsible for her family's death, or her father's hate?

"I want to *be*," she snapped. "I'm fine, okay?"

"Do you say that for me and the others around you to hear? Or do you say it for yourself? Why do you have to convince yourself that you're fine?" The man's eyes seemed to show empathy.

She sighed, exasperated. "Because I want to believe it. I want to know that all this time I've spent alone is fine. That I'm not so undesirable."

The man nodded. "You must examine your life, Brigit. What have you done that's so desirable? Why do you think you don't deserve to be alone?"

What the hell was wrong with this guy? Fortune tellers should be fun and casual tricksters. This guy pried, digging into her psyche and it started to sting.

"I've, well, I've done stuff. I helped raise my brother. I tried to keep in contact with my sister when my dad took her. I took over this stupid store for my mom. I've...I've..." What else?

What had she done that might be considered good or make someone want her? "I've tried, okay?" she shouted.

"You've lost hope." The man locked eyes with her.

Suddenly, everything inside Brigit turned to ice and flowed into her belly, an uncomfortable cascade of emotion.

"You gave up on life." He took a step back and began to pace around her. "You said, 'I am broken, I am lost, I am useless' and you believed it. You didn't care about your apartment, you hardly take care of poor Henry, you don't go out, you hate every-one, and you don't care that this is happening around you."

"Piss off," she hissed.

"You have dreamed all your life that someone would come and save you. When it wasn't your father, you gave up. You thought your mother too weak, so you pushed her away. You thought you were stronger than Mary, so you don't take her seri-ously. But you are so very jealous of her faith."

"What?" Her voice came out small and weak. She almost couldn't hear it over the rain.

"Mary has hopes and dreams. You don't. You gave up on dreaming, imagining a different future for yourself. You fed that to the dogs." He laughed, a dark, evil chuckle. "That's why you hate her."

"I don't hate Mary. She's my friend!" Her voice cracked. She started losing it. Becoming unable to control her emotions, reactions. This guy obviously wanted to drive her nuts. She couldn't snap out of it and make him leave. Like a heavy chain held her to the floor.

"And you know who else let you down?"

"No one let me down. I let *them* down..."

"Yes, very true." He smiled. "Ildanach."

She froze as he continued to walk circles around her. "How do you know about him?"

His dark chuckle gurgled up again. "That's a story you don't want to hear about, love. A long one. He made you angry, didn't he? He said insane things to you as though they were fact. You thought he was perfect. Everything you weren't, right? Joyful, funny, content, and excited about life. And he was pulling you with him. He was making your life interesting again. He was dancing you out of the hell you created, and you loved him for it."

The truth being spoken made it more real to Brigit. She hadn't been able to say why she loved Ildanach so much, and now she knew. Everything that man said was true. That's how she felt. Ildanach pulled her up and out of her depression and she hadn't even noticed. Mary had though. That's why she knew Brigit was ready to teach that class. She had seen the difference. Ildanach really had helped her. She had let her guard down and let someone help her.

"That doesn't make up for crazy talk," the man said, as though he heard her thoughts. "He's a liar, trying to get into your head. You need to push him away before he hurts you again. You know, in your heart, Brigit, that none of what he said was true. There's no way. Come on, love, you're smarter than that. You are a genius who knows how to live her own life."

"I want him," she whispered, hardly in control of her own thoughts now. A haze muffled her mind, a grey, dense haze she couldn't think past.

"No, you don't. You could never work through the lie he told. You are strong. You are fine."

He was right. A tear rolled down her face, and she nodded.

"I am fine. And I don't know why he said those things. Why would he do that?" She began to cry softly. She knew it all to be true. Ildanach played some cruel game on her. Getting into her life and emotions just to break her heart? Surely there were people out there who got off on hurting others. He had to be one of them. He was so cruel.

"I hate him," she sobbed. "I don't know why I let him into my life like I did. I kissed him, touched him."

"Because he made you think you were not fine. He lied to you like the snake he is. Manipulated you, made you the fool to laugh at.

"Brigit, my dear." He put his hand on her shoulder. "It is better to be alone and strong than to be someone else's fool. Listen to me. Hear my voice. Let me help you. All you have to do is say yes to me. Your soul is too dim for this world. Let me have it and I will keep it safe."

"My soul?" she asked, sniffing. "What do you mean?"

The man smiled. "Just say yes." His amulet glowed brighter now, yawning open ready to take something in. "Say you want me to help you. I will make everything fine."

She focused on his hand on her shoulder so much that she hardly noticed and didn't care that Henry leapt from his cage and scurried out the cracked window. She didn't know what he was up to as he had never been the running sort. All her attention focused on this strange old man and his amulet. And his words. She believed every one of them.

Henry dashed down the streets and into the sewers at top speed. When he ran, he moved faster than regular ferrets and knew the paths well. In a matter of minutes, he popped out of the storm drain near the junkyard. Robin saw him and knew him at once.

"Ildanach, it's Henry!" he called.

Ildanach was just leaving on his Ducati and stopped when he saw the ferret. The creature rushed to him and opened its beady eyes wider, showing him the scene it just witnessed. Anger pulsed into Ildanach's heart, mingled with fear.

"He has her again!" he roared. "Why can I never be with her when this happens?"

"Go!" Robin shouted. "You spent too long justifying yourself to Herne this morning, and now she's in danger. You have made your choice and I stand with you. Go!"

Ildanach revved the engine, spun on his back tire and raced into town. Too many times he had let Brigit die at the hands of Arawn. Not this time. And not ever again. Ever.

Chapter 23

The Story

"I thought I could make everything fine on my own," she said, all her worst memories bubbling to the front of her mind. Leaving her family, hating her father, ignoring her brother, moping for years in this shop, surrounded by things she had decided to hate. Getting involved with a man she did not understand. Putting her heart on the line like that. All that had got her was a broken heart and an aching chest, raptured with sobs.

"And you've tried so hard," Arawn cooed soothingly. He put his other hand on her shoulder so that he held her in place. "It's time you gave up. There is no shame in that. Your time is over. Why stay on this earth? You did well. Let it go and give up."

Just admitting that she wanted to be through with life would be easy. She didn't have to do anything about it. However, admitting to herself that, yes, she had screwed shit up couldn't hurt. After all, isn't that what they say? Admitting to something is the first step to healing. Maybe this guy just wanted to help.

She sighed deeply and wiped a tear away. "Yeah, I'd like to put this all behind me. You're right."

A manic smile cracked the man's face. His eyes glowed golden, and she swore a wolfish howl in the distance lilted on the air to her ears. There weren't wolves in the city. Wolves? She couldn't pull her eyes away from his. He suddenly looked familiar. Was he that guy who let his dog shit in her patch of grass every day for the last three months?

"Are you..." she began, but he cut her off.

"Look here." He pointed to his amulet, which really did glow now.

She gasped; her mind became instantly transfixed. Almost like comfortably zoning out. The kind where she couldn't pull her mind back so easily. What had she done? What had she said yes to and how had she gotten hypnotized now? The glow enticed her, pulling her in like a warm, welcoming light. It obscured all her vision now, changing the scenery around her.

In front of her a wide, stone arch, impossibly huge, yawned open. All around it, emitted a white light, a big expanse of nothing. She had to look into the arch where white veils hung, blowing in a soundless breeze. Mist cascaded around it, beneath it, and from it. It looked a little like what she imagined the gates of heaven to be like. Back when she believed in an afterlife.

Then a shape appeared in the archway behind the veil. She had to part the veil if she wanted to see who they were. The familiar shape made her heart leap. She had to see. Reaching out with a shaking hand, she parted the veil and looked into the beyond. Standing far off, swathed in golden light, stood her mother. She gasped. James stood beside her too, far away but completely visible.

"What is happening?" she said aloud but her voice came muffled, as though she had her ears covered. "Mom? James?"

They smiled, not speaking. Her mother tenderly put her arm around James and squeezed him. Her little brother raised his hand and waved. She took one step towards them. Her mother held up her hand, signaling her to stop, and slowly shook her head.

"Say something to me!" Brigit called out to them. "I've missed you. Are you alright?"

They both nodded, glowing and smiling.

In that instant, Brigit understood. They were fine. They were on the side of the world they believed in and were safe, together, and happy. And they did not blame her, hate her, and were not angry at her. Somehow, she knew she would not be allowed to join them.

"Why can't I come with you?" she asked. "I'm sorry for everything. Don't you want me, mom?"

Her mother replied with a pitying smile. James playfully crossed his arms and shook his head, his charming grin making her heart hurt. He flicked his head towards the world behind her: She had to go back and live her life. She had to be satisfied that they were all right and that they still loved her. They weren't letting her go yet. Something else had to be done.

"What do I have to do?" she asked. "I don't understand any of this."

Her mother gracefully placed her hands over her heart and mouthed one word: remember.

James cocked a half smile and tapped his temple knowingly at her. He winked and in a second, they were both gone. She stood alone in the soundless, white place between her world and the world beyond the veil. Her skin tingled with joy at being here, as if she had seen a familiar place she couldn't wait to get back to. She felt like someone waited for her, calling her name excitedly. Before her, a great light shone whiter and warmer than the glow of the doorway.

"Don't go towards the light," she said dully. "Then what do I do?" she shouted.

No one answered. She had to figure it out.

"I know this place," she said for a start. "I feel like I've been here before and I'm supposed to do something." She glanced around. "This is beyond the veil. Like in those stories. Or, not quite beyond the veil, but between, I think. That's why mom was here. This is her heaven."

She reached out, and the light warmed her skin. She gasped! As she reached her hand out, she saw her flesh glow. Glowed like that yoga instructor had. She was glowing!

A far-off tinkling of bells alerted her to the distance. She looked around. She knew that noise. High, tiny bells. She had had a silver anklet that made that noise when she danced.

"I don't dance," she said, confused. "Yes, I do. I did. When I came through the first time." She grasped her forehead. A slight ache started in her temples and spread over her skull. "I came over to find him. I came to find Ildanach! Ah!" She smiled, wide and open mouthed. "I remember!"

Brigit sat in her sylvan throne, running her fingers through her hair, which was pure, flowing fire. She gazed down through the veil at the fairy warrior. The one next in line to be guardian if Prince Pwyll ever returned behind the veil. Ildanach was strong and playful for a warrior. Not like his trainer Pwyll, who believed in stern discipline and silence. She secretly hoped that Ildanach would never become a guardian so that he could stay on this side, and she could continue to watch him.

One day, he went to the side of the mortals while Pwyll followed up some dark spirit movement. Brigit didn't think twice about following him over. She had a plan and wanted to test Ildanach. She took the mortal form of an old woman and followed the warrior as he went from settlement to settlement, checking on the mortals and exiling pesky sprites where he found them. She admired his work, but really had no love for the mortals as he did.

Using her goddess magic, she created a small home and garden in the woods and made herself the owner. Invoking the aid of a couple of sprites, she had them wreak havoc on her small hovel and called out for help. When Ildanach appeared, she said, "Oh, god of fairies, help me! These sprites will not leave my garden alone! They've spoiled all my vegetables and now I haven't any for the winter."

Ildanach used his runes and incantations to expel the spirits and then returned to the woman for the tribute. When mortals believed in the fairies, they paid tribute in a form of sacrifice or honor. The fairies drew their power from this love and worship, which allowed them to maintain nature and see that all was right.

"I have nothing," the old woman said, sadly. "The spirits have taken all my good food and I have no songs to sing for you. What shall I do?"

Ildanach considered. Pwyll would be furious if he left a

mortal uncharged and yet he didn't have it in his heart to take what she could not give.

"Your faith is your payment, lady," he said strongly. "I know the court will not be pleased. It is my duty to protect and serve you, and so I have and so I will again. I do not fear the wrath of the prince who trained me."

With these words, Brigit smiled and revealed herself as a beautiful young goddess. When Ildanach saw her and recognized her, he fell to his knees and begged for mercy.

"Gracious warrior," she said, kneeling with him in the forest, "your heart is too strong for punishment." She took his face in her hands and saw he was smiling.

"Looking on you would outweigh any punishment," he said in his cocky way. "This is a moment I will always carry with me, goddess."

"I was hoping you would carry *me*," she smiled. "If you can catch me, hunter!"

Giggling, she gathered her skirts and fled into the forest, singing the whole way. Ildanach took up his cloud and followed her, tracking her path. To test his pursuit, she opened the veil and fled inside. She watched from her throne and saw the warrior become dismayed. He searched for her for days and seemed to give up, still keeping an eye out.

While Pwyll was still away, Brigit came out again, tying silver bells around her ankles and teased Ildanach with weaving in and out of the veil, dancing to make the bells chime. He was a mischievous warrior and set up a diversion for her. Being the goddess of healing and life, she stopped to care for wounded animals or dying plants while adventuring to the mortal side of the veil.

One day, her bells giving her away as she danced through a field of flowers, she came upon a wounded weasel-like creature. His back leg had broken, and he tried desperately to hobble into his hole.

"Oh!" Brigit cooed, speaking to the poor thing. She had no powers in mortal form, and so she bound the leg as best she could. Grateful, the weasel ran onto her shoulders and tangled itself in the fire that was her hair. She giggled, petting it as it chattered and tickled. She recognized it now as one of the creatures who are as spirits; wise, cunning, and have a slight magic of their own. She was glad to have saved it.

Suddenly, long, strong fingers covered her eyes, and the scent of sweet smoke filled her nose.

"I've got you now, goddess!" called a triumphant voice. "Come in mortal form, have you?"

She tried to struggle away, but the man proved too strong. She grunted and kicked, falling backwards onto the man. He spun her around, pinning her to the ground, holding both her wrists in one hand. He gazed down at her with deep, dark eyes.

"We can only do what I have planned if I am mortal, hunter," she breathed, out of breath from struggling. She willingly submitted to his power; his playfulness charming, and yet strong and forceful. "So, you've caught me. What will you do with me now, hunter?"

"Whatever I please," he moaned, bending down and taking her mouth with his, hard and strong.

The scent of the flowers surrounded them, the sun warming them. She struggled again under his weight, trying to free her hands. He held on all the more tightly. She giggled as his kisses traveled down her neck, onto her shoulders, light as butterfly wings, then as deep and urgent as a hungry bite.

Deciding it was time to trade, she used all her weight to flip over, putting herself on top.

"Who watches the mortals while you romp in the woods, warrior?" She ripped his tunic open and leaned in to kiss his strong chest, trailing her hands up and down his muscled arms. "Why do you love them so?"

"It is my duty." He gasped as she lightly kissed his hips bones, grasping at his belt.

"And does duty mean so much to you?" she mocked, straightening up to straddle him. She threw one leg on either side of his hard thighs and ran her hands up and down his torso, lingering near his belt. "What of love, and living your own desires?"

He reached up, pulling her against him. Then his hands went to quick work on the laces trailing up and down her back. She rained kisses on his face and chest while his fingers worked urgently.

He moaned. "I cannot think of myself. I must be selfless and watch over those who cannot protect themselves."

She slipped out of her over layer and looked down at him, her breasts just visible under the thin fabric. His eyes ran over her, hungry and loving all at the same time.

"And what about what I want?" she asked softly. "What about me? Am I second to these mortals?"

He pulled her slowly down next to him and wrapped his arms around her, his hands on her chest. She moaned and leaned into his touch, starving for more.

"We could be together forever if I gave it up," he sighed. "I cannot. How can you not pity them? They are lowly, yes, but they give us our existence."

"They are feeding rats," she said harshly. Suddenly, the mood dissipated, and she sat still. "You do this every time. I do not understand this love you have for the mortals."

Ildanach didn't know what to say. He buried his face in her hair and pulled her closer, their nearly naked bodies melding into each other. He wrapped one leg around hers and pulled it back so he could move his hand between her legs. He stroked her gently.

"I cannot explain it, my love. You want for nothing so you cannot understand. I see their suffering; their hardships and I understand. I choose to love them even though they may be vile."

Guilt flooded the goddess in her mortal form. She could never be that selfless. In the few months she had chased this warrior, she had seen him display more power and gentleness than any other living creature.

"I want to be like you," she said at last. "Teach me to value mortals as you do. Teach me to love as you do."

He engulfed her in his embrace.

Ildanach and Brigit stayed together until the sun set. When they both returned to the veil, dark news awaited them.

"Arawn has escaped the underworld," Herne told the court. His great horned crown always demanded respect, but now his forceful tone was more so. "He has taken Prince Pwyll and slain him."

A gasp went up among the fairy court.

"Why?" a few uttered. Cries of "The devil!" cracked through the throne room.

"No!" Brigit cried out.

This meant that Ildanach would be sent to the other side of the veil forever. She could never see him again.

"I will go, of course," Ildanach said bravely to the court. "I understand my duty."

The morning he was to leave, Brigit went to him and begged him not to go.

Falling on her knees before the man she loved, she wept, "Please, don't do this, my love. Why do you wish to leave me?"

Ever brave, he answered, "It is not what I wish, it is what is right."

Panicking, she said, "Let me come with you. I know a spell only lovers can create that will bind Arawn again to his prison."

Ildanach frowned at his love. "You cannot come. You will be mortal. If Arawn finds you, he will take your soul. The soul of a goddess would empower him beyond anything I can fight."

"Then let us perform the spell before he finds us."

Not being able to persuade her otherwise, Ildanach traveled to the other side with Brigit attached at the hip. They had to make their way in mortal forms to the sacred stone circle where the magic flowed strongest and the veil thinnest. They took glow with them for Ildanach should he need to fight. Brigit took none.

When they arrived at the stones, darkness was already evident there.

"We must hurry," Brigit said, casting a circle around a stone table in the center. Ildanach watched for dark spirits, weary as they were. Though he saw nothing.

"Come, my love, and lie with me." She laid on the table and raised her skirts to welcome him. "We must make vows. To stay on this side, as mortals. Arawn will not walk this earth as long as we live."

"Brigit," Ildanach interjected, sadness weakening his eyes. "You are a goddess. You should not give up your life like this."

She took his face in her hands like she had so many times before. "For the mortals you love, my darling, I would give up more than I have. This is all I can do. And pray another after me does the same."

Holding on to his resolve, Ildanach mounted the table with his mortal goddess. They chanted, not knowing of the trap they had let themselves into.

A great grey host appeared out of the shadows, Arawn on his grey horse at the front. He cackled and raised his arms, calling up his hounds.

"Come for me as mortals?" he shouted. "Foolish lovers!"

The hounds leapt up from the smoke at the horses' hooves and charged to the table. Ildanach sprang to his feet, unsheathing his sword, protecting Brigit. He scanned the grey host, looking for a weak link. There were at least seven of them. He was just one.

Two hounds leapt at his face, their fiery fangs open wide, a burning maw searing his flesh as he just moved aside. Brigit rolled off the table, away from the host, and looked for a weapon. She would not go down without a fight. But she was mortal and had the boundaries of a mortal body. Arawn vanished from his steed and appeared behind her while Ildanach fought the hounds and other dark spirits.

Brigit heard him and turned to face her foe. "Stop us now, will you?"

"For eternity," Arawn hissed. "No one should be allowed to love like this."

He ripped a yellow orb from his neck and charged at Brigit, holding it out. She screamed and rolled to the side, just missing the soul-stealing amulet. Hearing her cry out, Ildanach turned and ran to her as Arawn gave chase. The dark spirit vanished and appeared so fast even Ildanach had a hard time keeping him in check.

Finally, Arawn revealed himself in a flash of light and grey smoke, shoving Brigit against one of the standing stores. She coughed out her air and her mind swam from hitting the stone. Ildanach ran to her, his sword poised to defend, but Arawn stood before her.

"Strike me down, warrior," he mocked. "Become the guardian you are meant to be! Be strong! Strike and save the mortals. End my suffering!"

Brigit shook, her eyes unfocused and dizzy. He could do it now. The grey host closed in and the hounds howled again. It was now or never. He had two seconds to decide.

With a savage yell, Ildanach thrust his great sword forward with all of his strength. His sword merely passed through a grey, thin smoke and into the warm flesh behind where Arawn had been standing.

Blood spattered his face and he blinked, seeing Brigit's wide, confused eyes in the dim light. She had opened her mouth to gasp, but no sound could emit. His sword had pierced her clean through.

"No!" he roared. He lunged to catch her as she fell, her body tiny and weak in his arms. "My love, forgive me!"

She gasped and held her stomach where the fatal wound rested. "Once more," she whispered in broken tones. She opened her hand and out fell the yellow orb. Her eyes glowed and then from them, a warm glowing stream flowed underneath her skin, down her neck, into the orb. "Once more, so mote it be."

Her eyes went dim.

Chapter 24
Bound, Shackled

Brigit couldn't see her store, even though she knew, beyond a doubt, that she stood in it. Everything around her shimmered golden, green, and sparkled. Far away, she saw a vision of a being she knew to be Herne. The horned god looked up, feeling her presence. He met her eyes over the distance, placed his hand over his heart, and bowed to her. She knew him. She smiled and nodded her head. They had spent many seasons together. He was a wise king and had shown her all the powers she possessed and how to use them to benefit the earth.

"I'd stay and catch up, my dear mentor," she said to him, "but I have a task to accomplish. Something I should have had the strength to do many thousands of years ago."

"I wish I could have seen you," Herne replied. His eyes were glad but full of melancholy. "We've missed you." One last bow of his head in her honor.

Brigit remembered everything. Her sylvan throne, her subjects, her nights spent sprinkling dew over the fields for the mortals to splash through in the morning. She remembered touching their crops, making them grow and thrive or fall ill. She had touched many a man, curing his illness; she had raised many fairy children in her court to be servants of nature and to help her with her tasks. She had an eternity of memories that flooded her mind. Her power surged back to her, asking her to be strong, calling her back to the other side of the veil. To be safe, to be a goddess again.

She refused. She must go and remain mortal and do what they needed to do so long ago. The world demanded her sacrifice. The mortals that Ildanach loved so much needed her just one last time. She would not be bestowing life on this day.

Besides, who wanted to live forever, anyway? Ildanach would part from her forever if she chose that. He was part of now. He was part of a single moment that she wanted to have.

His touches in the woods, his kisses amongst the stones, his panting in the fields of flowers where they would hide together - these things were forever. They would always have happened. She wanted today, this one forever. She wanted now. Nothing else mattered. Ever.

"Ildanach!" she said out loud. "I want hope and I want you. I have to believe in love to find it or else I can't see it!"

"You goddess-whore!" Arawn shouted, coming back into focus. "Take her, my hounds."

He signaled behind him where his hounds had been waiting. One growled, gnashing fiery teeth and took a step forward. It barked, harsh and loud, then yelped in pain. A smooth, iron stone lodge itself in its forehead, killing it instantly.

Brigit and Arawn looked behind them. A new hole had shattered her replaced window. A perfect, round hole. He was there! Ildanach's hat obscured his face as he loaded another stone into his sling.

"You've killed just one, guardian," Arawn shouted,

unsheathing his own iron blade. His skin hissed and sizzled from touching it. He didn't have the protection Ildanach did. "How will you take me and my pack: You never have before?"

"You look older than ever," Ildanach nodded, looking out from under the brim of his black hat. "Your power is weakening. You need to go back to your deep hell." He closed his sling and spun it. "And you've never pissed me off this much before."

Brigit begged him to look at her with her mind. She didn't have her powers. What could she do to help? There had to be something. Ildanach couldn't fight alone, she knew that for sure. She looked around. Surrounded by swords she constantly told people were magical, engraved with runes of fairy magic, she had options. They were no longer nonsense runes and inscriptions; suddenly, she realized she could read them! One had the name Goblin's Bane; another told a story about being a wolf slayer in the days of Beowulf. That one would do, inlaid with silver. She had seen silver do damage to a fairy in the past. Silver could be especially fatal to dark spirits.

She ran to the back wall where it hung. Arawn saw her run, commanded his dogs to Ildanach, and leapt after her. She ran to a rack of cloaks and hid inside, steadying them with her hands. Peeking out, she saw Arawn stop and look for her. Glancing behind, she saw Ildanach engage the hounds. He had killed one more with his sling and now attacked with his iron blade. Blood covered his handsome face, but could not hide his snarl.

"You have never won against me, bitch. What makes you think that this time is any different?" Arawn hissed, his eyes scanning for her.

She had never been this Brigit before, that's what.

"Ah!" she screamed, leaping out.

The enemy whirled around, slashing sloppily. He missed, and she ducked behind the magic mirror. Her mind raced as she thought of a plan. She had to hurry.

She dashed out and grabbed the sword from the wall, slashing as she spun around. Arawn jumped back, his grey robes just meeting the blade as she screamed like a warrior maiden. She slashed once more, making him leap back again. She felt like her old self again. She had fought wars before. Some on this earth and some in the fairy world. She was not weak. She never had been. She had just not made the right decisions when it mattered. Not again.

Taking Arawn's distraction as his hounds yelped, Brigit ducked back to her new bookshelf and grabbed the spell books she had scoffed at before. If anything turned out to be real, these would. She had only one second to glance at the index before Arawn was upon her again. He thrust his arm out, using his powers to conjure chains that flew towards her.

She screamed, ducking, the chains striking a body that dodged in front of her. Ildanach grunted as the magic iron wrapped around the wrist of the arm he thrust out to protect her. Arawn pulled, trying to yank him in, but Ildanach proved too strong. He held his ground, his arms flexed powerfully.

"A good try, chain warden," Ildanach growled. To Brigit, he called, "I'll distract him, you find the spell." He ran towards their hated enemy and kicked him back with one powerful, booted foot.

"Why do you always try to be so brave?" she said, flipping madly through the book, her sword still in one hand. The chains linking Ildanach to Arawn clinked and clanged against the floor as they fought.

"I thought you liked when I was brave," Ildanach grunted again, clashing blades with Arawn.

"No, I like it when you're safe." She rolled her eyes, still looking.

"No, no, I clearly recall one harvest when you were very upset with me for not helping the mortals. And after, you covered the land in a frost too!" He spun away from a stroke that would have been fatal.

"My hounds!" Arawn cried, seeing the blood all over Ildanach.

"It was needed to purge the land, I told you," Brigit defended. She tore a page, crumpled it, and threw it to Ildanach. This was the one.

He caught it and spun away to get a glance at it before tossing it away.

"Stay back!" Arawn shouted, conjuring more flying chains toward Brigit. They hit her full in the face, wrapping around her neck. Not being a fairy yet, they did not burn her, but they were tight and heavy. She coughed and stumbled.

"Hey!" Ildanach shouted. Arawn turned.

Ildanach's hand bled where he had cut it to draw blood.

"Magic spell ink," he smirked. "Fairy blood is pretty powerful."

"Cocky bastard," Arawn sneered back. "You haven't everything needed to write that spell and send me away. You've failed every time! Do you know how often that has been? Do you know how many mortal souls are wandering this earth thanks to your failures?"

"I never had this particular Brigit with me," he smirked

again, panting from exertion. "She's a little more something, that's for sure."

"And never will again," Arawn pulled Brigit's chain, yanking her towards him.

She jumped to give herself more power, thrusting out with her great wolf-slaying sword. Arawn saw it and spun out of the way, landing himself right on top of the spell symbol Ildanach had drawn with his own blood on the floor. Panicked, the dark spirit looked up just long enough to see Ildanach position behind the partly broken mirror.

Brigit caught sight of Arawn in the mirror as he appeared in the fairy world: his smooth face was sharp and angled in rage, eyes glowing teal. This world aged him. His long, white hair whipped around him as he spun to find a weakness in the sigil on the floor.

"I won't go back to your prison!" he screamed. Behind him, angry spirits – no doubt a few of his victims – massed together in the reflection.

The mirror, inscribed with the second part of the spell, tilted. Ildanach shoved it forward onto him. The remaining bits inside the frame didn't shatter when it hit him. Instead, Arawn slipped through it like a doorway and the mirror crashed, glittering into pieces once it hit the floor.

Brigit stood, panting and rubbing her neck where the chain had bruised her. It was gone, along with its master. She stared at her broken reflection in the mirror shards. Before her memories had returned, she had known that mirrors were said to be portals into another world. Now she knew.

She looked up at the man she had loved. The man she did love. The man she had let down for an eternity. She had never wanted to rip her clothes off and make love so fiercely before. But there were things that needed to be said.

"I am sorry I don't keep blessed ink in the store," she choked out.

Ildanach looked down at his bloodied palm, dropping his iron blade. "If we don't seal him away forever, it will heal," he said softly. An unexpected tragic note cracked his voice.

A longing and a pain she knew too well. They had never come this close before to locking Arawn away. They had just moments before he came back through another portal into this world.

Brigit understood what he said. She didn't want to say the words, though. She was weak, after all. She sealed her lips. She had him now. Why couldn't they just run? Just leave, back behind the veil and be in exile? She wanted him, and she wanted him forever. Not just one mortal lifetime.

Tears filled her eyes and she sobbed. She couldn't even go to him. She longed to touch him, but it seemed wrong if they were not going to do what needed to be done.

Ildanach looked up at her. "We must decide. Now. Can you choose to die?"

Chapter 25

Last First Touch

Had she never remembered any of it, she would have said yes right away. She had already decided to give up. This wasn't that. This was not giving up. This choice would let her be with the man she loved. It would also be her last chance to live.

"How can you ask me to make this choice now when all I want to do is touch you for the first time?" she asked. Her heart, despite the happy reunion, began to break. The need to reach out to him, to pull him to her, and press herself into him caused her utter agony. If she did, even just one caress, she would never want to let him go. She would deny the mortals the safety they so needed. She would betray her fairy people.

The large fairy clock behind her ticked louder than ever. They had to hurry. She had to decide.

"Please, say something," she begged.

Ildanach's dark eyes set in a strong glower, not sad or fearful like hers. "I have so much to say that I'm afraid if I begin, I will never stop. My dear Brigit, I have lived for this moment. Even now, my heart races because I have never made it this far."

"Why did you always look for me?" She didn't understand why he kept on living. "You could have left me, given up, appointed a new guardian and found another, more worthy love behind the veil. You could have done anything, even just stopped looking for me after so many deaths."

He took one step towards her over the broken glass. She stepped back, afraid that if he got too close, she'd throw herself into his arms and complete the spell.

"How can you ask that?" He spread his long fingers, enticing her.

She wanted them on her, all over, touching, loving, feeling - making her gasp with a pleasure she could not even remember now.

He winced in hidden pain. "There is nowhere on this earth, or in our world, I could go where I didn't feel you in my heart. I did run from you. I tried to hide, but I could not leave you. I could not breathe without the thought of you in my mind. I could not fight without knowing that someday I would see you again. Every time I walked down the dark streets, my eyes grew tired from searching for you. They grew darker every year. I did not know my heart could long for you as hard as it did. And every time I found you, I thought I'd die from gladness. And every time I let you down, I wanted death. I knew there was only one way to find you forever. That," his eyes blazed with passion and intensity, "is why I never gave up. I would rather spend one last life with you than forever losing you."

Brigit shook so much her breath came in gasps. Her entire frame vibrated with fear and anticipation.

"One last first touch," she said hoarsely. Her throat clenched tight, not letting the words out. She took in every detail of Ildanach. His bleeding hand, the healing scars on his chest, his long powerful legs that she now remembered so intimately. His silken hair and his face that used to smile. He glowed now, with fairy power inside of him that she did not have. Her glow was purely internal; she had given up her goddess-like powers many lifetimes ago for this one purpose. She could either take them up once again or leave them, dying a mortal in due time.

She smiled, the tears finally splashing down her face. "How can I say no? After all you've done. Waiting for me, finding me, saving me, and loving me every time. I remember them all. You never, ever gave up. Ildanach, my love, I will live and die with you if you will have me one last time."

She held out her arms and he rushed to her, taking her into a powerful and savage embrace. She gave herself up into the first kisses they had shared in this life. She grasped at every part of him, desperate to know him again. He rained kisses and caresses onto her face and then her neck. Their passion drew them to the floor. Brigit fought to get a tapestry under them as he pulled her onto a rune-carved table much like the ones from their past.

He made quick work of her blouse and she his coat and shirt. His chest was just as she remembered only more scarred. She ran her fingers over his newer wounds gently, then kissed them. His fingers gripped her hair.

Unable to wait any longer, she let him remove her jeans and his own. They locked eyes as at last they were joined, moving in perfect rhythm, with each other for the last first time. The intensity grew, the heat between them like a fiery ocean, pulsing and flowing. Brigit grasped his shoulders as he squeezed her hips, pulling himself deeper into her as she matched his movements. The fever spiked, their sweat mingled in trickling droplets, and Brigit gasped, her toes clenching, and she shook in passionate fury. Her nails dug into Ildanach as she felt him release. They quaked and her vision blurred.

United at last, Ildanach panted and laid down next to her, his face buried in her hair. She wrapped her elbow around his neck and pressed him against her, not wanting to be any further apart. Skin against skin didn't seem close enough. The tapestry stuck to their sweating bodies as they caught their breath.

Brigit took up Ildananch's wounded hand and kissed it. "You're not healing." She whispered.

He propped himself up on his elbow and looked towards the shattered glass. No sign or mist, no howl from a hound, and no clicking of hooves could be heard. Arawn was gone, bound away in the underworld at last.

"And I never will heal," he said. He clenched his fist, drawing blood again. "Never again."

Brigit kissed his sad mouth. "But I am healing. I feel it. And so is this world." She closed her eyes and inhaled deeply. "The souls are leaving, retreating behind the veil now. They are safe and glad." She opened her eyes and took his wounded hand. "You have saved them."

"And so have you. What you have done, no other goddess would have. Giving yourself to a lowly guardian, sacrificing your life – these are things none can do but you."

"It was because of you," she said softly. "You showed me that these humans are worth saving. Your love for them inspired me to understand. And I love you so much, I had to try. You are no lowly guardian. You are this earth's savior. No guardian would give his life for them as you have done."

"Only because this last life is with you. I am the fortunate one; I have a goddess."

"And I have a warrior."

She laid her head on his chest and listened to his heartbeat. His scent, warmth, and life rhythm soothed to her. She closed her eyes, knowing everything would be alright. What felt like for the first time in her life, she closed her eyes with no fear of death.

"Oh yes, I believe in magic now," she giggled. "That was magic."

Ildanach laughed into the dim light. His laugh made her curl her toes in giddiness and snuggle even closer. His was the most beautiful smile she had ever seen, and she was glad he wore it often.

"I will wonder for some time, I think, if I did the right thing," he said at length.

Brigit knew the answer to that right away. "You have. You have done more than your share. It is time for you to focus on this life now. Your only life."

A small, cold, trickle went down into her stomach now as she said these words, making them a reality for her too.

"My only life," she said almost too softly to be heard.

Her one thousand lives played before her eyes one last time. Each life in a new age, a new world. And this would now be her last.

Ildanach rose and pulled her up too. He tucked her hair behind one ear and then cupped her chin in his hands. He rubbed her tears away with his thumb gently.

"Our life. The one we chose. And no matter what, I will love you for eternity." He kissed her softly this time, his urgency not gone, just satisfied.

"We don't have eternity," she said, smiling despite herself.

Ildanach shook his head, glowing in a human way from his beautiful smile, just like she loved. "I don't care about the boundaries of time. I will love you forever and no one will stop me. Ever."

She wrapped her arms around him and they lay together once more, surrounded by the runes and the silence. "Then I will love you for eternity, too. In this life, the next, and everything after."

To Be
Continued...

"Brigit! Mary called, running down the street, the familiar, struggling ferret clutched in her hands. "Henry escaped! But it's okay, I caught him sniffing around my shop's front door."

She stopped when a weird glow inside the store caught her eye before she made it to the door. The light was oddly human-shaped, moving in a horizontal, waving motion. She recognized the wide-brimmed hat. Her mouth dropped and she gasped in shock. How could Brigit hook up with Ildanach and not tell her? And the glowing?

Exclaiming a myriad of Egyptian gods, she took two, enraged steps towards the door.

"I wouldn't," a deep, smooth voice warned her from behind.

Spinning around, Henry still in her hands, her breath caught in her throat. A tall man with a dark skin tone leaned against a light post. When she blinked, for just one second as her eyes opened, she swore she saw antlers covered in hanging moss towering over his head. She blinked rapidly trying to see them, shaking her head.

"Who are you?" she asked lightly, pretending she had not stared at this stranger.

"I have many names." He smiled at her kindly, like he knew her. "I wanted to thank you for watching over our goddess.

Mortals have always played a part in our histories, but you..."
His smile sweetened and he tilted his head. "You are special,
aren't you?"

Mary's eyes widened at the flattering words, and she scoffed
dryly. To distract herself, she pet Henry roughly.

"He doesn't like that," the man offered when the ferret
moaned and narrowed his eyes.

"Goddess?" Mary asked, repeating his word. "I'm sorry, but
there is a glowing man in my friend's shop and I have to go."

She made to turn away, but the man called her middle
name. *Rhiannon!* This time, his voice echoed like it came from
down a long tunnel.

"Did you move your lips?" She glared at him again,
watching closely. "How did you know that's my name?".

Changeling child, his voice whispered, clearly in her mind.
Is that you?

Out loud he said, "You could hear me?" Above his head, the
vanishing antlers almost wavered into solid view as she struggled to see them.

Mary swallowed hard, her mouth still open. "No one has
called me that in a long time. Do I know you?"

Above them, the moon broke through the clouds, shining
down on them. As it hit the pavement, illuminating Mary, she
looked down and saw that she cast no shadow in the moonlight:
where her shadow should have been, an illuminated outline of
her lay.

Rhiannon? the horned god gasped.

Rhiannon will awaken in *Unshackled Moon: Goddess Among Us Book 2*

Abi has been a writer all her life, but is a mentor at heart. When she is not writing, you can find her slaying enemies online or hunting for the next bohemian adventure. She has published works of fiction, poetry, academia, and even won awards for her short stories in science fiction and horror.

Abi is also a proud mom of two... ferrets! She live streams on Twitch where you can enjoy her terrible gaming skills and join the live discussion. She works part-time as a freelance ghostwriter, editor, and audiobook narrator, hoping to one day make these passions her full-time job. She currently resides in Kansas.

She is one of nine children--all who share the creative spark.

Find Abi online at: www.abigaillinhardt.com

Also by Abigail Linhardt

Season of the Runer Book I: The Trial of Two
Season of the Tuner Book II: Sojourn
Why They Killed: A Waksha Virus Novelette
Golmasiah: The Outerwinds
Prince of Midwest (coming July 2022)